GW00384611

Salute to Bl....... .

Roderic Jeffries

© Roderic Jeffries 1954

Roderic Jeffries has asserted his rights under the Copyright, Design and Patents Act, 1988, to be identified as the author of this work.

This edition published in 1954 by Hutchinson.
This edition published in 2017 by Endeavour Press Ltd.

Table of Contents

Chapter One

Richard Verrell somewhat gloomily spooned up a mouthful of ice cream. The ice cream was not at fault, for it had been prepared by the cook herself and was superb in texture and taste. Nor was he depressed by the fact that Diana Freshman sat opposite him. Anyone who partnered her might count himself lucky, since she possessed the unusual combination of looks and intelligence. What really disturbed him was the fact that his host, Sir Edward, was in full spate.

Sir Edward was a V.I.P. The newspapers liked him because he had news value. His was not a case of rags to riches. His father had left him close on a quarter of a million pounds; the product of many complicated deals on the Stock Exchange. A chip of the old block, as it were, the son lost no time in making that sum double itself, and then double itself once more. Before long he was so rich that he could not avoid becoming richer. He made more, much more, and still more by methods so strictly within the letter of the law that his legal advisers must have been worth the large sums they were paid. He was, in fact, one of the wonders of modern business. No amount of displeasure, rage or enquiry ever threw the least shadow of doubt on his transparent honesty.

"My contention is, that the modern generation, brought up on cheap films, cheap books, comics and tinned foods, receives absolutely no culture. It cannot appreciate what is good, or differentiate from what is bad." Sir Edward glared at his guest.

"Yes," Verrell dutifully replied. He had met Diana at the home of mutual friends, enjoyed her company on several occasions since, and had been delighted to accept an invitation to stay at her home for the week-end. He realized now he had made a bad mistake.

"What is more, it must not be thrown at them from all directions. If a man has never eaten caviar, and you want to introduce him to it, it's no good making him eat a couple of pounds of the stuff at first go."

Verrell nodded his head, hid a smile as he glimpsed Diana's wink; a conspiratorial gesture.

"A man with money has an obligation to his country; to bring it culture. That's why I started my small collection…"

Sir Edward paused, disappointed. Nobody had contradicted the word 'small': neither his guest, who, even if he were a writer, ought to try and show some manners; nor his daughter, who should have had at least that much filial respect.

He continued, a trifle sharply: "My orders were that, as far as possible, the finest examples of the arts should be brought together so that the general public might have the opportunity of realizing what they have been missing all these years, and to stimulate their interest in art."

"Have you seen the collection, Richard?" Diana asked. Experience had taught her that once the floodgates were open the best course was to allow the waters to gush out as speedily as possible.

"I'm sorry to say I haven't. As a matter of fact, I didn't know it was open to the public."

"Not know it was open to the public!" Sir Edward slammed his napkin down on the table. "That is what I have to fight all the time. Apathy. No other expression for it. Public apathy. Mark my words, it will lead to our ruin." He was a strange person to speak about ruin. "Why didn't you know it was open?"

"All the descriptions I have seen have referred to it as a private collection."

"Pah! You might have tried to find out "

"Why on earth should he, Daddy?" Diana tried to contain her impatience. "You can't expect people to spend their lives checking up references in guide books."

"As I've told you before, Diana, my museum is more than something you can read about in guide books. It is a collection that has taken years to assemble, and incidentally — " he coughed with becoming modestf, "a remarkably large sum of money."

The fact that his money had not been mis-spent would doubtless bring comfort to the heart of many a disillusioned investor, Verrell reflected.

Sir Edward continued: "It has been so arranged, catalogued and described that a study of it…"

Verrell listened because there was no other course open to him. Earlier on, Diana and he had arranged to enjoy an evening's dancing at a nearby country club, but it was becoming increasingly obvious that they were in for a disappointment. Culture, spelled with a capital K, held the field.

Diana was equally annoyed. Even more so, indeed. Her father was almost everything a father should be in respect of a dress allowance, and odd and not inexpensive items of jewellery, for instance, but an evening spent in the company of Richard was eminently desirable. He was good-looking, disarmingly youthful when he smiled, and had a pair of wicked brown eyes which made her breathe with quickened interest whenever she met their caressing glance. But the quality which distinguished him from the usual run of her friends, and which attracted her more than any other, was an indefinable air of devil-may-care adventure, a manifestation of the spirit which had fired buccaneers in the past.

Which was hardly surprising since Verrell was even better known to the public as the notorious Blackshirt, the mysterious and elusive cracksman who had plagued the police for many years.

Happily unaware of this second existence of her favoured guest, Diana glanced at him with hopeless resignation and shrugged her shoulders.

The butler entered, and patiently waited for an opportunity to break into a monologue which he had heard so often before he could, if necessary, have acted as quite a useful prompter.

Sir Edward paused to draw breath. Beach snatched at *the* proffered opening.

"Will you take coffee in the drawing-room, sir?"

"Yes, Beach, and bring in the brandy at the same time. Shall we move?" He stood up. "After we've digested the meal I'll take you round, Verrell, and show you my collection. Of course you'd like to see it." The remark was more of a challenge than a question.

"Please."

"Good. If you'll excuse me for a moment, I have a 'phone call to make. Carry on there, Diana, don't wait for me." He disappeared through one door as the others moved into the drawing-room.

"Sorry about this, Richard. And just when we were off to the club."

"We can make it some other time."

"I'll take a raincheck on that." They reached the coffee. "How do you like it, black or white?"

"White, please." He offered her a cigarette, took one himself. "Next time you're doing nothing."

She laughed. "I'm going to be brazen. Name the night, and I'll make a point of being free. You're too good a dancer to pass up."

He grinned. "I'll come to you for a reference."

Sir Edward soon joined them. His strong, somewhat heavy face expressed satisfaction.

"Sorry to have rushed off like that. Had to get hold of my stockbroker. Some shares of mine are a little tricky. Here's a tip for you. If you have any Telmont shares, sell them."

The hint did not surprise Verrell. The shares had been in the news for several days — coupled with the name of Sir Edward Freshman.

"Sometimes wonder why I don't retire," Sir Edward carried on as he poured our two generous brandies. "Everything one makes is swallowed up by taxes these days; much of it for the National Health. Can't understand the idea of giving so much away. Easy come, easy go. Make 'em earn their luxuries, is my idea. Then, perhaps, those damned Inland Revenue chaps wouldn't be so cursed curious." The Revenue Inspectors had long been interested in Sir Edward's income, but they had never worsted his accountants.

"I see the papers are hinting at another rise in the income tax to try and balance the budget." Verrell thought it quite a change to hear his own voice.

"I'd give them balance," Sir Edward commented darkly.

Diana broke in. "More coffee, Richard?" Her voice was as impatient as her expression.

"Not for me, thanks, Diana. One's my limit after dinner."

Like daughter, like father. Sir Edward became impatient.

"Finish your drink, and we'll go along to the collection. You coming too, Diana?"

"Don't think so. I must write some letters before I go to bed tonight. I'll join you later."

Sir Edward led the way through the house. Terrance Hall was a large Georgian house built in the shape of the letter E. The main part, designed for the owner's private use, contained all the living rooms. The east wing housed the servants' hall and bedrooms; but the west wing, hitherto neglected by the series of past owners, had been chosen by Sir Edward to become not only a home for his art collection but at the same time a permanent and sumptuous monument to his greathearted patriotism.

The entrance to the wing was at the far end of a wide passage which ran the length of the main building. The heavy oak door was strongly bolted, and double-locked.

"This is the only way into the wing from the main building," Sir Edward explained as he unlocked the door. "Similarly, of course, it would be a way into the main building from the wing for unwanted intruders, if I hadn't taken all precautions."

They passed through the doorway into a square marble entrance hall. In addition to the door connecting with the main building there was another on their right, and swing doors opposite them, on the far side of the hall.

He indicated the door on the right with a wave of his plump soft hand. "Public come in this way. About fifty a day on the average. Not enough."

"It's some little way out of London," Verrell mildly excused.

"If people can't be bothered to travel twenty-five miles to see my collection they don't deserve to be treated as civilized beings."

They crossed the entrance hall, passed through the swing doors. A man, who had been sitting on the farther side, immediately stood up.

" 'Evening, sir."

" 'Evening, Trapes. Everything all right?"

"Yes, sir. Everything in order."

Verrell surreptitiously inspected the guard. The man looked a tough character. He had solid shoulders and a thickset trunk, and his face was in keeping, flat-featured, heavy-jowled. A whistle and lanyard hung round his neck. Round his waist was strapped a gun-holster, with the butt of a heavy automatic very much in evidence. The effect was ridiculous, ostentatious, but quite in conformity with Sir Edward's absurd pretensions.

"Unusual to see arms in this country," he commented casually.

"Certainly it is. Took some straight talking to get the police permit, too."

Having passed by two side passages they walked along a short corridor, at the far end of which was another pair of swing doors.

"Ever had trouble?" Verrell asked. He could not imagine the police would permit the carrying of arms unless there was good reason.

"Once. A few months ago. Someone tried to break in during the night. The alarm soon sent him scurrying off, but after that I wasn't taking any more chances. I doubled the night guard, and asked the police for a firearms licence."

Sir Edward pushed open one of the swing doors for Verrell to pass through into the exhibition proper. To Verrell's surprise it was immediately obvious that considerable taste had been shown in arranging the collection in spite of its being such a hodge-podge.

Sir Edward was well and truly wound up. His descriptions and history of each exhibit were interminably long and scrupulously detailed. Before each hitherto unmentioned artist a stop had to be made in order that his guest might be regaled with boring anecdotes of the painter himself, the school to which he had belonged, his individual method of execution, and his private life.

Nor was Verrell spared this ordeal when they passed on to the few choice pieces of Queen Anne and Regency furniture, the first edition Shakespeare, some illuminated manuscripts, a Gideon Bible, some Paul Storr silver, the incredibly ancient Chinese scrolls, the jewelled weapons — it was a feast that sickened through overrichness.

But, eventually, he was rewarded. They reached a showcase filled with examples of the goldsmith's art. Most of the exhibits were worth more than the average man earned in a IO

lifetime, but there was one piece in particular — a pearl pendant set with exquisite taste in delicate filigree; a gossamer web.

"Some valuable stuff in here, Verrell. Worth darned near as much as the rest of the collection. That crown, for instance. Came out of Russia "

Verrell was not listening. He had eyes only for that pendant. That pendant...

" — and as for that ruby," Sir Edward drooled on, "it has a history going back to the early Ottoman Empire " He broke off. "Aren't you listening?" he asked testily.

"I was wondering how you can bear not to lock them in a safe each night. To have all this wealth lying around would give me the jitters."

He could not have said anything better calculated to please Sir Edward. "They *are* in a safe — as good as!" he purred. "This place is burglar-proof. *I* saw to that when I first started the Freshman collection."

Verrell grinned. How often had he heard similar words? How often had Blackshirt proved the boast unjustified?

"Ha! See by your face you think I'm talking nonsense. Listen to me. There's only one way into this wing of the house. By way of the entrance hall. How many doors did you see in that hall just now — apart from the swing doors into this room?"

"Two," Verrell obediently answered. "The public entrance and the door into the main building."

"Right. And what was this side of the first swing doors? An armed man. Right?"

"Yes, but "

"I know, I know. An armed man can be knocked out. Then what? The burglar walks along the passage to the next lot of doors. While he does that, what happens? He passes an invisible electric ray which would set off an alarm loud enough to wake the dead: an alarm which would not only warn the second armed guard that an intruder had forced his way in, but would also wake all of us in the main building. To say nothing of the servants as well."

"Hum!" exclaimed Verrell thoughtfully.

"And mind you, there are other invisible rays."

"The windows "

"The windows! Look at them, man, look at them! See those iron bars. D'you think you could cut through them?"

Verrell had a set of tools that would do just that, but he kept the information to himself.

"Suppose you did cut through them. The moment you pushed your head through — ping! goes the alarm. Suppose you can prevent that; suppose you can actually lay a hand on any one of the exhibits — well, hear for yourself!"

Sir Edward moved one of the paintings. The noise was deafening.

"I see what you mean," Verrell agreed as soon as the alarm stopped.

Sir Edward laughed. "Look at the windows."

Verrell looked. Every window was now concealed behind a heavy steel shutter.

"D'you see? You'd be caught like a rat in a trap, for the doors are shuttered, too. Well, what do you think of the chances of stealing anything from the Freshman collection? Eh, what do you think?"

Verrell shrugged. "Impossible, of course," he admitted with ostentatious admiration. For all that he glanced sideways. If that pearl pendant didn't soon change ownership it wouldn't be for lack of Blackshirt's trying.

Chapter Two

Verrell looked at his watch. Two o'clock. Time to move. He stubbed out his cigarette, stood up, flexed his muscles. He turned his travelling-case upside down on the bed, gave each of the four metal studs a push and a twist. The false bottom sprang open, to disclose his famous black shirt, hood, gloves and belt of tools.

The collection of tools was the product of many years' experience. Made of the finest steel, there were few safes which, in his skilled hands, they could not open. He buckled the belt round his waist, then slipped on the shirt which had earned him his nickname — all that the police had to identify him by — a pair of evening-dress trousers and dinner-jacket, and lastly, the black hood and black gloves. Now he was no more than a black shadow, invisible among the normal black shadows of the night, only to be glimpsed if and when a beam of light fell directly upon him.

He switched off the bedroom lights; waited, listening. Not until his ears satisfied him that he alone was up and about in that part of the house did he open the door and move out into the passage. As he moved silently along the pile carpet he heard a peculiar muffled sound from one of the bedrooms, and identified it as Sir Edward's gentle snoring. He moved on towards the stairs, but took care, en route, to step carefully over a board which he had earlier noted had a tendency to creak loudly.

He reached the door which connected the house with the west wing. It was bolted and locked, but the keys were still in the locks. Using the greatest caution he unbolted and unlocked the door, eased it open so that he could see into the marble entrance hall.

The guard was there, standing by a small alcove in the wall which had been concealed by a carved wooden panel when Blackshirt had first seen the hall; now the panel was open, and in it, he could see, were all the necessary paraphernalia for making tea or coffee.

The guard was making coffee; his fourth cup that night. Soon it was ready, but not for drinking: it was too hot in spite of all his noisy blowing.

At last the coffee was sufficiently cool. The guard took a long and noisy swallow, then replaced the cup in the alcove. Blackshirt thought the man was on the point of walking away, but no. He took a cigarette out, lit it, and exhaled with obvious satisfaction. After a few puffs he finished the coffee, and reluctantly closed the panel. His smoking grew faster. He was feeling irritable, wondering just why he had taken a job that meant his staying awake while the rest of the world could relax in sleep. For two pins he'd throw it up and try for something more congenial.

This was wishful thinking, as he well knew. The pay was good; better than he could hope to get elsewhere. Besides, the old boy saw to it that he ate well, allowed him and the other guards a quota of free cigarettes each week. In return, all he had to do was to make certain that nobody succeeded in passing through the swing doors. A simple enough job, if only it weren't so sleep-making. In spite of the four cups of coffee he could feel a familiar sensation creeping over his skull; it seemed to start at the back and work forward to his eyes. He knew that craving for sleep of old, and how quickly he could become a victim to it. He began to walk up and down the small space, pacing it with the methodical precision of a seaman keeping watch on the bridge.

It did not take Blackshirt long to realize the reason for the precision which stopped the guard well short of the swing doors leading to the collection. A good six feet short. Somewhere within those last six feet was the invisible ray which could be switched on or off only at a point situated somewhere in the main building — for, having set off the alarm earlier on, Sir Edward had had to telephone through to Beach to switch it off; proof enough that it should not be possible for the alarm to be tampered with in the wing.

Look at the problem as he would, he could see no way into the room housing the collection — at least, not by way of the entrance hall. He had not anticipated that there would be, but he never left anything to chance. Now only three possibilities were left. To enter from below, from above, and through the windows.

He closed, relocked and rebolted the door, and made his way to the main entrance of the house. As he had expected, this too was locked, bolted and barred, but it is always easy to get out from the inside. Before doing so he did not neglect the elementary precaution of oiling the hinges and bolts, to prevent even that faintest squeal.

The windows were large, high up the walls, designed for their light-giving properties rather than for their proper place in the scheme of architecture. Only by standing on tip-toe would even a tall man be able to reach the sills.

He eyed the moon-reflecting windows thoughtfully. He would need either a ladder or a pair of steps to examine one at close quarters. He did not much care for the idea, largely due to the fact that, on one of his less successful forays, he had tried to place a ladder against the wall of a house with such a noisy result that he had had to run hell-for-leather to escape capture. But, if a ladder was really necessary…

He found a gardener's shed behind the rockery at the back of the house. Inside were several ladders, and two step-ladders. He chose the larger of the step-ladders, and carried it round to the west wing. With great care he stood the steps close to the wall, and mounted them.

The moon was setting. There was not enough light to enable even his keen eyes to observe the finer details of the window. He was compelled to use his torch, but he adjusted the shutter until it emitted no more than a pinhead of light.

The bars, he saw, were set deep into the brickwork, so close together that they formed a formidable barrier that would require an acetylene burner to dispose of it in reasonable time; filing, even with his fine tools, would take far too long. Nor was there any sign of rust which might have weakened some of the bars. Ignoring the additional hazards of the alarm and the steel shutters, it was obviously stupid to consider the windows as a possible means of ingress.

He returned the step-ladder to the shed, then paused for a moment to review the situation. It was certainly beginning to look as though he would be forced to acknowledge the truth of Sir Edward's words. Before he was ready to do that, however, there were still the floor and the roof to investigate. Who could say that it might not be possible to find a weakness there? It would not be the first time that a house had had every door double-locked and a window carelessly left half-open.

The cellars took some finding, but eventually he discovered a door in the main building which led below. He descended the wooden staircase, and moved along a brick passage which appeared to lead in the direction of the west wing. Farther along, a brick wall prevented any further advance, and satisfied him that the cellar beneath the west wing had been completely walled-up.

From the depths to the heights. He moved up to the topmost floor where he found stairs leading to an attic. Investigation of this disclosed a skylight, thick with dust. He opened it and peered out across the roof. The night was by now too dark to allow him to see more than a matter of inches. It would be a risky proceeding to use his torch — some patrolling police-constable, perhaps a mile away, might see the flash, and have his curiosity aroused — but the chance had to be taken.

A brief flash of his light enabled him to see that the roof was sufficiently shallow to be crossed without the use of a rope or ladder. He swung himself out, and made his way crab wise to the west wing roof.

Not without having experienced a few anxious moments he reached the roof of the wing. A moment's examination proved that Sir Edward was no boaster. Each individual tile had been set in cement, making the roof as strong as the rest of the building. Anytime the Bank of England had a surplus amount of gold sculling around, it could be stored in the exhibition below with complete confidence!

He retraced his steps, and after a breathless moment on the main roof, when he unwittingly put his weight on some dried moss which broke away, he regained the attic, and returned to his bedroom.

There he allowed himself a last cigarette before getting into bed — at an hour when it was often his host's habit to wake up and worry about the state of the stock market. As he idly watched the smoke eddy and vanish, he reviewed his nocturnal exploration of the house. Reason reassured him that he had missed nothing, overlooked no loop-hole in the defences. Not until he had stubbed out the cigarette, changed into a pair of really brilliant pyjamas, climbed into the bed — it was one of those high, old-fashioned beds that needed climbing into — pulled the bedclothes over him, and switched off the bedside light, not until that moment did he accept his findings as final.

"The old blighter's right," he muttered in disgust. "The place is completely, absolutely, and in every blooming way burglar-proof."

Blackshirt had met his match.

Chapter Three

"Good morning. Sleep well?"

Diana was already half-way through her breakfast when Verrell reached the dining-room. On Sundays the first meal was an elastic affair; household and guests chose their own hour for taking it.

"Like a log. Asleep almost as soon as my head touched the pillow," he answered quite truthfully.

"Good. Whatever else this place has or hasn't got, the beds are comfortable. I saw to that. Help yourself to what you want. Ham or tongue on the sideboard, toast and marmalade here. If you want bacon and eggs and kidney, give the bell a tinkle."

"Thanks. Ham looks good to me. I'm not one of your true-bred Englishmen who requires bacon and eggs seven days a week to make him happy."

"Good for you. What shall we do after breakfast? Sit around, read the newspapers, and join the moans every time something goes down a sixteenth? Or dash off somewhere?"

He grinned. "From the tone of your voice, there's no choice. Where do we go?" He was more than ready to fall in with any suggestion. Diana was an asset in any circumstances: she was young, nice to look at and gay. What more could a man want? Besides, another full-length dose of her father and his Art might see him dropping off to sleep in self-defence.

"Care to take me out to lunch? There's a place not so far away, where they really do put on a good show. Afterwards we could go for a hike through Rothsey Park. The way they keep their gardens up is absolutely staggering."

"Somebody has a business expense-account I But the idea sounds a hundred per cent."

"Good. Next thing is to tell the staff that they've only one to cope with for lunch."

They were interrupted by the arrival of Sir Edward, who said good morning quickly before returning to the newspaper he had been reading as he entered the room.

Diana asked him what he would like, translated an unintelligible grunt as ham and tongue, and passed some to him.

"Richard and I are going out today, darling, so we won't be in for lunch. All right by you?"

"Yes," he muttered absently.

Apart from one or two comments regarding the alarming uncertainty of the world in general, the rest of the meal was taken in silence.

Verrell returned to his flat in London on Monday morning. Roberts, his valet, opened the door.

"Good morning, sir, did you have a pleasant week-end?"

"Fine, thanks. Anything happen?"

"Nothing important, sir. There are three letters on the table. There was also a 'phone call thirty minutes ago from the publishers."

"Did they say what about?"

"Yes, sir. They want you to get in touch with them about the dust-jacket for your new book."

"Not again! Thought we'd settled that days ago."

"The artist wants to know whether the heroine is to wear mink or sable. She was wearing mink on the visual, but he thinks sable would look better. Does it affect the story if he makes it sable?"

"How about some coffee first, before I ring them?"

"I'll make some right away, sir." Roberts left the study and went into the kitchen.

Verrell watched him go and, in passing, thought of the day, many years ago, when the valet, without references, had applied for the situation. He had taken Roberts on, only to learn later that there had been no references because the man had just finished serving a sentence for robbery, yet neither man had ever had cause to regret the arrangement.

He opened the letters; sighed on finding that two were begging circulars, probably sent to him on the principle that every author makes a small fortune. The third was from a friend on holiday in the south of Italy. He finished reading it as Roberts brought in the coffee. Twenty minutes later he was back at work. The week-end was over.

So he thought! But not for long. He was half-way through a manuscript, and had arrived at a sticky patch. He had hoped that the break would see him over it, but after fifteen minutes' concentration he was still dull-witted. The words refused to come, probably because he could not keep his mind on his work. He could not forget the Freshman collection. In particular, he could not forget that exquisite pendant.

On Sunday morning he had gone to sleep convinced that nothing could be done about obtaining the pendant. Now he had his doubts. What one man could make, another could break. Surely there must be some method of forcing an entry into the exhibition without raising the entire neighbourhood?

Were the windows quite so well guarded as he believed? Perhaps a close daylight inspection would reveal a flaw. Was there no way of getting past the guard? There might be, but what about the invisible ray? Suppose he succeeded in getting past the guard? How could he first locate and then avoid it before it set off the alarm?

The more thought he gave to the puzzle, the gloomier he became. He hated to be beaten, but it was becoming increasingly clear that there was no alternative to sitting still and admitting defeat; admit that the man of culture had been correct. It was damnably galling...

So it was impossible! Did that mean that he shouldn't go for a short car drive, say in the general direction of the Freshman home, and have a pint or two? Of all places to discover everything about the lives of local inhabitants, a pub was the best. Even if, at times, the information became a trifle garbled in the telling.

"I'm going out to lunch," he called out.

His valet appeared. "Very good, sir." This despite the fact that he had been about to serve the meal. There was a certain Jeeves-like quality about Roberts which overrode anything from an earthquake to a general election.

Verrell drove along densely crowded streets in the direction of Oxford. It was with a sigh of relief that he finally reached the green of the countryside. He loved cities, the heart of cities, but there was something about the monotonous streets of Suburbia which always made him think of the saying: There, but for the grace of God...'

The Claymore Arms stood at cross-roads some three miles from the Freshman house. It was a brick edifice, *circa* the thirties, and looked it. As much in keeping with the countryside as a thistle in a field of com.

The private bar was almost empty, in contrast to the public bar, a pertinent indication of the countryman's ingrained carefulness. By the time he had taken the top off his beer he was the only customer left in the private bar.

"Nice day, for a change, sir," remarked the publican.

"Weather hasn't been all that bad lately."

" 'Tain't been all that good neither, sir. Not round these parts. Ground can't take no more water, it's had so much. Just passing through, sir?" He spread his elbows on the bar, and prepared to talk or listen as required.

"That's all. Having a look at the countryside, and what's in it. Several interesting places round here, aren't there?"

"Depends on what you calls interesting. Some good views up along them hills at the back. Come a fine day and you can see as far as Cheescum." The landlord went on to extol the neighbourhood, which appeared to have no peer in all the realm. When Verrell called for another pint the gregarious host accepted the offer of same. It was not difficult to steer the conversation round to the Freshman collection.

"I ain't never seen it myself, though me old girl has and says it's something. I ain't one of these political troublemakers, but somehow it doesn't seem right to me that so much money should be locked up by a private person in such things. Now, if he'd bought all the land that was offered when the house was sold to him, and farmed it as it should be farmed, well, that's my idea of how money should be used."

Verrell chuckled. Culture was not quite so important, it seemed, as Sir Edward believed.

"And all the trouble he goes to, to keep anyone from helping himself to them pictures and things! Believe it or believe it not, the whole blooming works is wired up like a kid's Christmas tree. And guards! It's lousy with them. The only good thing you can say about them is that they comes in here for a drink now and again."

Later, Verrell sat down to a meal, provided by the publican's wife; a meal of substantial proportions if not of much dignity. Meanwhile, he had learned one fact, and one fact only. Attached to the house was a private electric power generator, held in reserve against a power cut. Somebody had certainly been thorough. Far too thorough.

After lunch he drove awhile, parked his car out of sight and looked about for a suitable spot from which he could study the house. His binocular-case hung round his neck, a last gamble as it were, carried in the hope that from a distance he might discover a weak chink in the house's defences. He skirted a small copse of trees, and settled down.

The wing showed up clearly through the high-power lenses. Ten minutes' observation was sufficient to prove that reason had been more justified than hope — as far as could be seen from where he was. A fighter up to the last ditch, he rose and moved on to another spot from which he would be able to study the other side of the house. He found one, some distance away, but when, once more, he lowered the binoculars it was with the disappointing realization that he must definitely and finally admit defeat.

It was with something approaching consternation, therefore, that Verrell read an account the following morning of a burglary which had taken place the previous evening at Terrance Hall.

A painting had been stolen from the well-known Freshman collection.

He stared at the headlines in astonishment, then disbelief. Somebody must have made a mistake. It wasn't possible to steal from the Freshman collection. It just wasn't possible. Hadn't Blackshirt investigated, and decided that the collection was burglar-proof? And if he couldn't break in — and out! — who could? It just wasn't possible.

But there was no mistake. He read on, feeling very much like the scientist who had stated that there could never be an H-bomb because it was a scientific impossibility.

The facts as reported in the newspaper only deepened the mystery. Briefly, they stated that a man had entered the building which housed the collection, and then had vanished like a puff of smoke. With him had gone a painting by Van Dyck.

There was only one thing left for Verrell to do. He ignored his resolution to spend the day working, and drove to Terrance Hall.

The butler, a trifle distraught, opened the door.

"Good morning, sir. For a moment I thought you were another policeman/' His tone of voice showed what he thought of the recent intrusions.

"Is Miss Freshman in?"

"Yes, sir. Will you wait in here, and Til announce you?"

He was shown into the drawing-room. Not for the first time he admired the tapestries at either end; two of the surviving Mortlakes.

"Richard! What a lovely surprise. I thought Beach must be suffering from the general confusion when he gave your name. Coffee?"

"Sounds perfect."

"What brings you here to see me?" Diana's eyes twinkled. She had more than half an idea why, but was determined to make his explanation difficult.

He decided to be frank — almost! "I wondered if you would care to come out somewhere this evening. To cancel the raincheck."

"I'd love to," she answered promptly. "Why didn't you 'phone? It would have saved your coming out all this way."

"As a matter of fact, I read about your burglary in the evening papers. It sounded such an impossible story I couldn't believe it. Since I intended asking you out tonight, I thought I might just as well come and see for myself how untrue the report was. Or if it wasn't, to offer you my sympathies."

She laughed delightedly. "You're a fraud, Richard. If it hadn't happened there wouldn't have been any invitation."

He had the grace to grin shamefacedly. "I must say that it all sounded a little peculiar. That's the trouble about writing books. Read about a real mystery, and you start trying to solve the puzzle. The report I read was obviously up the pole."

"Since it brought you here maybe it has done some good after all," she said cheerfully. "Anything to get away from the horde of police father has called in."

"Any progress yet?"

"How can there be? It's all impossible."

"How do you mean, impossible?"

She was interrupted by the arrival of Beach with the coffee, but as soon as he had gone she turned to Verrell. "Before I answer, will you stay to lunch?"

"Is that blackmail?"

"Absolutely," she admitted unblushingly.

"If it's not barging in — especially on a day like this."

"Of course it isn't. So that is settled, and now I can put you out of your agony. You probably remember that the museum — that's what I always call it — is open to the public every day until six."

He nodded.

"Last evening, about five-thirty, Johns and Trapes were on guard, Johns looking, as he always does, like a cross between a commando and a particularly nasty fuzzy-wuzzy. They were talking together — it was almost time for the changeover — in the entrance hall when Trapes went through the first lot of swing doors to get a packet of cigarettes out of his overcoat which he had hung up. A few moments later a visitor entered the entrance hall from the outside door, and asked Johns whether there was time to look round the collection. Johns told him less than half an hour, but the man said that that was time enough, and went on through the swing doors."

"Good job your father didn't hear the visitor say half an hour was time enough to see the collection."

Diana laughed. "Yes, isn't it? Anyway, just about three minutes later, according to the two guards, the alarm was set off. You can imagine the to-do. Bells loud enough to wake the dead, shutters dropping down in all directions, father rushing along with a twelve-bore, ready to blast away at anything and everything. Police were called, the alarm was switched off and the shutters raised so that the bobby could go in and arrest the man " She paused. "Give me a cigarette."

He offered her one, took one himself.

"Go on."

She raised her elegant eyebrows. "Go on? But that's all."

"All my foot!"

She relented. "Well, almost all. When the police searched the place they found it as empty of people as it had been all day."

"It was all imagination?"

"You might think so, but imagination doesn't set off alarms, nor does it pinch paintings."

"There really was one stolen?"

"Yes."

Verrell digested the facts of the story. They did not make sense.

"What about the windows?"

"Untouched. Besides, only a fly could get through the bars."

"They hadn't been filed or anything?"

"No."

"But — but "

She chuckled. "Quite! It couldn't have happened. That's what the dear inspector keeps saying. The only trouble is that it did!"

He drank his coffee, but without properly tasting it. Maybe his self-esteem need not suffer. All a burglar had to do, obviously, was to become invisible.

"How did the chap escape?"

"He didn't."

"You mean, he was arrested?"

"I don't."

"Then he is still there?"

"Where?"

"Hidden somewhere."

"He might be, at that — if there was anything or anywhere to hide in, which there isn't; and if the entire police force of the county hadn't been buzzing around ever since the alarm went off."

"What about the picture? Has that gone too?"

"Every square inch of it."

"And the frame?"

"Ditto."

"Then the man, the picture and the frame must all have dematerialized, or whatever the word is."

Diana looked disappointed. "Frankly, Richard, I was looking for something better than that from you. You know, 24

something like walking through a wall and rebuilding it after one.

'That's too simple. Have the police any theories?"

"They hadn't at breakfast-time, which made father even more short-tempered than usual at that awful hour. How about our going along to have a word with the inspector? Then you can check on whether I have been telling you a lot of womanly nonsense."

Verrell grinned. As a matter of fact, he *had* been thinking just that.

Together they walked down the corridor, past the guard who muttered a weary 'good morning', and entered the exhibition-room.

Three men were present. Two were sitting at ease on one of the settees provided for the comfort of visitors, the third was staring at the far wall where most of the paintings were displayed. His gaze was held by a blank space.

The two men stood up and the elder greeted Diana in a somewhat wary fashion.

"Richard, this is Inspector Stevens. Mr. Verrell has come along to solve the mystery for you," she added brightly.

The poor man was unable to manage a smile, and his companion was the first to speak. "The writer, sir?"

Verrell nodded.

A muttered sentence which could have been, 'My God! this does it,' tailed off at a withering glance from the inspector.

"No luck?" asked Diana after an uncomfortable pause.

"No, miss, no luck. And as I was saying to the sergeant, we're not going to get any, either."

Verrell offered cigarettes in an effort to ease the tension. "I gather it's a bit of a problem."

"I've been in the Force for more years than I can remember, sir. I've seen harmless little men do murder, and whisky-sodden brutes act like heroes: I've seen blind beggars with better sight than mine, and barristers with cardboard soles to their shoes... but never before have I come across a theft which couldn't have happened!"

"Maybe it didn't," muttered the sergeant. "Maybe we'll all wake up in a minute."

"I gather that the object stolen was a painting."

"It was. Two foot by two of canvas, and the frame, vanished with the man who stole it."

"Did it hang over there, where the constable is looking for something; spiders, perhaps?"

The inspector was too worried to consider the point. "Yes, and the moment the picture was moved, off went the alarm and down came the shutters. If one of these pictures is moved so much as an inch, within three seconds this whole room is boxed in as tight as you like."

"No thief could have reached more than half-way to a window in that time. Although even had he reached one, the bars look over-solid to me."

"Take more than a crowbar to shift them. No thief got out that way."

"Nor could he have reached the door."

"That's right, sir." The sergeant's voice suggested he had heard that remark before. "And there were two guards along the corridor. About all we can do now is work out how long it takes to fly to the ceiling."

Verrell was baffled. Diana's account of the theft had been correct. Far too correct. Blackshirt was obviously outclassed. He couldn't work miracles. Wasn't up to date. "There's only one possible solution," he muttered more to himself than to the forbearing policemen.

Their look was a clear indication of what he might do with his solution. He refused to be put off.

"There must be a secret passage through one of these walls."

"Richard, you're a genius," cried Diana. "Why hasn't anyone thought of that?"

The inspector eased his collar with his forefinger. "We checked on that, miss, within ten minutes of our arrival. We've consulted the architect's plans, checked every inch of the walls and floor, inside and out, and there is no priest's-hole, secret passage, or anything else."

"There must be, or else it isn't possible."

"There aren't, and it isn't," he retorted somewhat nettled.

"What about finger-prints?" Diana was hot on the scent.

Verrell noticed the agonized expressions of the other two. "Glad it's not my job," he remarked soothingly. "Bit difficult to persuade the Big Noise that the theft just couldn't be."

"We get used to it." The inspector was a philosopher. "No doubt, the Chief will have an answer. Come to that, sir, as a writer perhaps you can suggest what we should do next? Suppose you were a crook, how would you manage to disappear in the middle of the floor?"

It was all very well for the inspector to ask him how he would have stolen the picture! Hadn't he already decided that it wasn't possible to steal a small pendant that could be dropped into a pocket? If the pendant couldn't be stolen, what about a framed picture, two-by-two in size? Yet someone had succeeded in making it vanish. And to make the theft even more incredible, he, the unknown, had taken only three seconds to achieve the impossible.

"All I can think of at the moment," he said at last, "is that the picture must be hidden somewhere..."

The inspector merely waved his hand round. That was all he needed to do.

"Never mind," said Diana soothingly. "Maybe Scotland Yard will be able to help you."

Verrell saw the twinkle in her eyes, and promised himself that he would tick her off later for being so unkind. After all, the three policemen were trying!

The inspector looked as though he were tossing up a number of years in the Force, his future pension, and a few other things against the satisfaction of saying what he was thinking. The pension won. He even managed a sickly smile.

The constable detached himself from his study of a blank wall, and walked smartly across to the inspector.

"What shall I do now, sir?"

Once more there was a silent struggle in the inspector's mind before the constable was given a reply considerably more polite than the circumstances warranted.

"Have you a description of the man?" Verrell asked the inspector.

The inspector shook his head with a savage gesture.

"They saw him go by. Oh yes! First Johns, who was by the stove, fixing up a cup of coffee for himself, and then the other bloke who was taking some fags out of his jacket. What was he like? Well, that was easy. He was tall; about five feet six. He had a round face that was square in appearance. His black hair was chestnut in colour. He was dressed in a grey suit that was practically brown "

He turned to Diana. "I'm sorry, Miss Freshman. This business is getting me down. The only really reliable information about him that we can hang on to amounts to the fact that he had two eyes, two legs, two arms, and didn't use a crutch."

Diana and Verrell left the three policemen to their miseries, and returned to the main building. As they passed through the entrance hall Verrell touched her arm.

"One minute, Diana." He turned to the guard who was standing by the public entrance-door. "Are you Johns?"

"Yes, sir."

"Damn' peculiar, this business. Cigarette?"

"If Miss Freshman doesn't mind." He took one, lit it. "It is and all. What annoys me is that it was me who let the fellow through."

"Couldn't very well stop him, could you? Did he look the type who goes around stealing pictures?"

"Didn't give me that impression. As a matter of fact I didn't take much notice of him, me being busy with my coffee. Just a quick glance to see he weren't carrying no case, stick or umbrella. We don't want nothing smashed here."

"The inspector said you couldn't give much of a description of the man, but it's never easy to do that even when you have had a good look." There must have been something about the thief to remember, Verrell was convinced, that a little encouragement and quiet reflection might bring back.

The guard gestured apologetically. "It's more than I can do, sir. Never was any good at remembering faces. I doubt whether I'd recognize his photo if I was shown it."

"You'd do that right enough," Verrell encouraged. "Surprising how much one can remember without realizing it."

"I dare say you're right, sir."

He chuckled. "But you still have your doubts? How long after the man had gone in did the alarm start?"

"Difficult to say. My mate had gone along that side passage there, to get a packet of fags from his coat, and he must have been gone between three and four minutes, I'd say. The bloke arrived just as Trapes was walking away, and the alarm went off just as he came back. So it can't have been more than four 28 minutes. That's what I told the inspector anyway, and I ain't had cause to think twice."

"Of course not. Four minutes. Just time to go in and pick the one piece he had chosen. Why that particular painting, Diana?"

"Haven't a clue, except that it must have been worth a mint of money. Daddy never bought anything that didn't cost him the earth."

"Was it worth as much as some of that jewellery? Jewellery can be split up, but a painting can't. It would be a hell's bells of a job trying to sell it, now that its theft has been publicized. Why, some of the stones in the jewellery case must be worth ten times as much."

"Perhaps he had a market already lined up."

"Must have, I'd say, unless he was nuts." He shrugged. "One thing is certain. It's not much use considering that aspect of the theft until someone can find out how it all happened." He turned to Johns again. "Have you any ideas?"

"No, sir, I ain't. If I believed in magic I'd say that's how the picture was stolen."

"Try that one on the inspector. I think he'd appreciate it."

"Let's go," suggested Diana. "Getting near lunch-time, and I want a cocktail first."

They returned to the main building, as mystified as ever. They left behind them three policemen who had almost reached the point of believing in ghosts or goblins or poltergeists or demons.

Chapter Four

The meal was good. A soup of some brilliance was followed by lobster and a mayonnaise which had never seen the inside of a bottle. An excellent salad, and to finish with a *negre-en-chemise*. It was with a feeling of great contentment that Verrell replaced his napkin and followed Diana into the next room.

"What will you have with coffee, Richard? We have most liqueurs in that cupboard/1 "Are you having one?"

"Most certainly. If you really want to be a dear you can pour me out a Kiimmel; then choose what you'd like."

"I hear and obey."

He was pouring out the drinks when Sir Edward Freshman arrived.

"You're here! Thought I recognized your car. Come to see what all this ridiculous nonsense is about, I suppose." "He came to see me," exclaimed Diana pertly.

Her father snorted, caustically asked if there were any lunch left.

"I doubt it, but cook will soon knock something up. You didn't say you were coming back."

"Do I have to say when I'm returning to my own house to eat my own food, served by my staff?"

"My, we are in a paddy! Can't you unload those shares?" It was clear to Verrell that, in his home, father was not quite the power he was outside.

"Damn it! How many more times do I have to tell you I sell shares? I don't unload them." His stormy glance dared the others to cough.

They managed to remain silent.

"I came back to see what the police are going to do with the criminal who had the impudence to steal one of my paintings."

"They've caught someone then?" The other two spoke together.

"I damned well hope so for their sake! They've had all morning to do it in."

"We went along before lunch," said his daughter quietly, "and up to then they hadn't solved anything."

Sir Edward threw his paper to the floor. "Taxes, taxes, taxes. We pay them morning, noon and night for an efficient police force. And when something happens, what is the result? Absolutely nothing. I'll get Barker to ask a question in the House. I'll write to the Chief Constable. I'll be damned if they get away with this."

Diana had rung for Beach who arrived in time for the last 30 half of the indictment. He stood quietly until certain it was over, then spoke. "You rang, sir?"

"I want some lunch," Sir Edward retorted.

"There's cold meat — unless you'd prefer something like eggs?" suggested Diana.

"Never mind what, so long as I can have something," retorted her father. "First I want a stiff whisky. Then I'll go and have a talk with this half-baked inspector."

The butler left. Sir Edward poured out the promised stiff one, drank it quickly. He merely grunted when the other two decided to accompany him to the 'museum'.

In the last half-hour the inspector had reported to his superior. He was, therefore, not in the best of humours. The newcomer's first broadside effectively dispelled any remaining vestige of joy.

"Is it true nothing's been done about finding out who committed this outrage? Is it?"

"No, sir, we "

"You know who the criminal is?"

"No, sir, but "

"Never mind the rest. We'll start making certain we get some action."

"Perhaps, sir, you'd be good enough to suggest what we should do?" The inspector threw discretion aside.

Sir Edward flushed slightly. "You'll kindly refrain from "

Diana came to the rescue. On this occasion her sympathies lay with the police. "Don't be so impatient, Daddy, they're doing their best."

Verrell waited for further explosions, was mildly astonished when they did not come. Freshman contented himself with glaring at his daughter, then stalked across to the wall from which the painting had been removed. He regarded the blank space, hands behind his back.

"Come on, Richard, let's console the poor dear. Must be like losing a favourite tooth."

The inspector wondered whether he ought to thank Miss Freshman, correctly decided to hold his tongue. He went out and together with his two companions examined the outside wall for the third time.

Diana linked her arm through her father's. "Cheer up, it can't be all that bad. Suppose you'd lost several things instead of just the one?"

"My God! Just like your mother. Fracture an arm, and she'd say 'Aren't you lucky, might have broken your neck!' "

"You musn't indulge in these tantrums on an empty stomach. I'm sure it'll give you ulcers."

Sir Edward clearly indicated a certain regret that his daughter had not disappeared instead of the painting. "Don't talk about things you don't understand," he snapped.

"It's filthy luck," soothed Verrell, "but I take it the insurance will cover the loss."

"I wish people wouldn't damn well take things for granted all the time."

"There's no need to be rude to Richard too."

"Very well. For your information the insurance will not cover the loss."

"Why on earth not?" asked his daughter. "The whole lot's covered for anything anybody could possibly suggest. Don't you let them get away with that."

"Weren't you covered for theft?" asked Verrell.

"Yes."

"Very well then, father dear, what on earth are you complaining about? One Van Dyck stolen, one claim for thousands of pounds."

"It wasn't a Van Dyck," he contradicted.

"Wasn't a… I can remember when you bought it. Paid a record sum for it."

Her father swung round, his face etched into grim and faintly unpleasant lines. "I paid a record sum. And do you know what it was worth? Fifty pounds, maybe a hundred! The damned thing was a fake."

She gasped. "How do you know? When did you find out?"

"Where did I put that cigar?" Ignoring the prominent NO SMOKING signs he reached in his pocket. "I bought it in an auction as a genuine\Van Dyck. Paid a hell of a lot for it. Arranged to insure it and the company sent an expert down to check. After half an hour's puddling around he said he wanted to take it away. Said in his opinion it wasn't a Van Dyck at all, but was by that Bassete man."

Verrell's mind clicked. During the war, while France was occupied, the Germans had been assiduous in collecting — by one means or another — valuable paintings. A man named Bassete had sold them several Van Dycks. At the end of the occupation he was charged with having been a collaborationist. His defence was novel. He claimed to have painted these 'Old Masters' himself, thereby swindling the Germans. Regrettably, at the same time, he had also 'swindled' many an art critic who had rhapsodized over the newly-discovered works.

"What was the result of the check?" asked Verrell.

"After a hell of a lot of fuss and bother they came along and told me they'd insure it for a hundred and not a penny more. They'd proved conclusively it was a Bassete, having traced it right back to the chap who originally bought it, a German general."

"Couldn't you get your money back from the auctioneers?" asked Diana.

The silence was heavy. The sale had been well publicized. Also the fact that Sir Edward Freshman was a considerable connoisseur and art critic in his own right, owning one of the finest private collections in the country. It was hardly the moment to admit that he had been most horribly stung. Even if it only went to show that he could be bracketed with ninety-nine per cent of the critics. It had been a case of pay up and keep quiet.

"At least that means you've got one thing to be thankful about. Nothing of value has gone!"

Her father groaned. "For God's sake stop telling me I'm better off now than I was."

"I was only offering a little sympathy."

Father and daughter exchanged several more pleasantries. Verrell hardly heard them. He was in the past. Something was trying to sort itself out in his mind. Something that intuition told him was the key to the question of why the thief had taken but one painting — a false one at that.

Had the thief known it was a fake? Possibly not — probably yes. The answer at that point was not particularly important. But what was the name which kept evading his tongue? On the point of admitting defeat, it came.

"Was the German general's name von Steiner?" he asked abruptly. "The general who bought this painting from Bassete?"

"Uh?" Freshman stopped telling his daughter just how like her mother she was, tried to concentrate on the question. "What did you say?"

Verrell repeated the question.

"Something like that. Got shot. Damned good job. Teach him to buy fake paintings."

The pieces seemed to match, to fit the pattern. For a moment he wondered if he were being too fanciful; but many a fancy of his had turned out to be sense.

Von Steiner had been even more unpopular than other generals in occupied France, due to the fact that he had organized reprisals with typical Nazi thoroughness at the slightest hint of trouble. He did not wait until the trouble materialized. It was never quite certain for how many deaths he was responsible.

He had another side to his character. He was a patron of the arts — hence his purchase of the Bassete Wan Dyck'. His patronage extended farther: to cover everything of value. By his orders houses, *chateaux*, museums in the area he commanded were pillaged, and the valuables ecorted to the magnificent home he had chosen as headquarters.

When the war had reached the stage of imminent invasion von Steiner showed an unpatriotic — but accurate — assessment of the situation. He gathered together the best of what he had stolen, and arranged for its conveyance to a safer spot. That much was known. Where the loot was hidden was not. Five paintings he had sent back to his family in Germany, but nothing more from his collection. At about the same time he also sent a letter, later found, addressed to his wife and telling her to take every care of the paintings since they were worth more than might appear. This had always been interpreted as his belief that their value would greatly increase after the war.

No one was left to contradict this belief. Von Steiner had been killed by a strafing allied plane at the time of the Normandy landings. Later, his family received the business end of a bomb while visiting friends.

After the armistice, Allied officers had found the Bassete paintings in von Steiner's Berlin home and in due course they had been sold by auction. As for the rest of the loot, numerous efforts were made to find it, but without success.

It was here that Verreirs mind leapt from the realm of known fact to uncharted guesswork. The loot must have been well hidden because no hint of its whereabouts had leaked out. Other caches had been found, but not von Steiner's. The General must almost certainly have left a record, but all that had been found were the Bassete paintings.

Could they be more than just brilliant fakes? Could they be a link? With mounting excitement Verrell felt certain they could be. It explained why only one painting had been stolen from Freshman's collection; why so much else of greater value had been overlooked.

"When you come back you might say where you've been!" Diana was smiling at him.

"Sorry. I was miles away."

"Stale news. I asked a question twice and the net result was you continued to stare vaguely into space. Suddenly remembered something you ought to have done? Or has the solution of this problem come to the famous writer like a flash of lightning cleaving the shades of night... how's that for a simile?"

He grinned. "What did you call it?... Sorry to report neither of your inspired solutions is right. Just had an idea for my next chapter. Forgive me — what were you asking?"

"What time do we move tonight?"

He dragged his mind back to the more mundane aspects of]ife. "Doubt if we want to get there until after ten. Cabaret show is at midnight."

"Now we know why we're going. Lots of tableaux I suppose, charming girls sporting something less than a Bikini. Ah, well, men will be men." Although she spoke sorrowfully, her eyes sparkled with mischief.

He looked round the room. "Your father left?"

"While you were examining the atoms prancing around in front of your nose. Poor dear couldn't stand it any longer and had to go somewhere to blow off a little steam. To come to more important matters — what do we do now? There are a few hours before we need change. How about a swim?"

"No costume."

"We'll search through some of Daddy's. Thank goodness he hasn't yet developed a corporation."

"In that case I'm with you."

"Good. Get away from this place filled with so much sorrow and ashes of policemen's hopes... One of these days I shall write a book." She laughed as she led the way. "No need to say it. I can tell by your expression what you're thinking."

Diana was wrong. Most ungallantly Verrell was back on the engrossing subject of von Steiner.

The cabaret fitted Diana's description. Delightful young ladies in various stages of undress fluttered round the tiny dancing-floor, or sat with rock-like stillness, according to how much or how little they were wearing.

By two o'clock they had had enough and left. Verrell drove Diana back to her London flat.

"Good night, Richard, and many thanks. Wish we had a burglary every day to draw you up to Terrance Hall."

"For the last time, it was the other way round."

"You make a terrible liar." The door cut off her light laughter.

He returned to his car and drove slowly to his flat. A pleasant day, taken all in all. Diana — a perfect companion: and a first class mystery. Had he been asked in which order he would place the two delights, he would have been hard put to answer honestly. So pleased with life was he, that he tried singing. Previous efforts should have dissuaded him.

He entered his flat. Although it was late he resolved to enjoy one last cigarette while he sat in his favourite armchair and tried to pick holes in the ideas which were crowding his mind. He had lighted the cigarette, but not sat down, when the telephone rang.

"Hullo."

"Is that the Electricity Board?"

"No."

"It isn't! Damn it, that's the second time I've got the wrong number. I do hope I didn't wake you up."

"Not quite." Something was worrying him.

"Sorry and all that. I was working late and some idiot decided to cut off the electricity just as I reached a crucial point in my work. Masses of calculations spread all over the 36

table. By the time I get back to them I shan't know where I am."

Verrell disliked wrong numbers. This feeling grew to almost personal hatred when the man at the other end insisted on reciting his life-history. "Really?"

"I say, could you possibly tell me..."

Reaction was slow. His intuition had been right. The click of his door as it was opened made him spin round. Two men stood there, scarves wrapped round their faces. In the hand of one, a gun. In the hand of the other, a leather cosh.

"Put the 'phone down gently, brother." A vicious, uneducated voice.

Verrell did as he was bid.

"That's a good boy. Now back up against the wall, and keep your hands away from your pockets. Don't move too suddenly or this thing might go off." He indicated the gun.

"Don't hold it so stiffly then," suggested Verrell, "or the kick will break your wrist."

'Susie' — as Verrell irrationally christened him, probably because of his near-black eyes — was startled. He was unused to having his threats treated with levity. A trifle uncertainly he moved forward into the centre of the room. His companion moved with him.

"We're going to have a look around."

"By all means! If you want a guide I'll do my best."

"We might do — don't want to go away empty-handed."

Verrell laughed easily. "You've got the wrong place! Once upon a time I had a gold cigarette-case — you'll find it at that convenient little place round the corner called a pawnshop."

'Susie' grunted. "Nice to find someone with a sense of humour."

Verrell turned and regarded the other man. Although half his face was covered, what was left was sufficient to show he was a thug pure and simple. "Bet that's more than your friend has," he said cheerfully.

"Shall I croak him?" The second intruder spoke for the first time.

'Susie' ignored the rough query. "Care to tell us where you keep your valuables?"

"Wish I could!"

"Might be better if you did."

"Threats!" said Verrell quietly. "So we are playing rough! What will you do? Put me on the rack — or try red-hot pincers. Neither original, but both supposed to be very effective."

'Susie' swore. It was difficult for him to keep his temper with his mocking inquisitor, who was supposed to be an intended victim transfixed with fear. "If you want to play it the rough way, that suits us."

Verrell was curious. The men might have picked on his flat by chance. It was doubtful. But the solution of that problem could wait. He was faced with a more pressing one. He flexed his feet, straightened out his balance.

"Beginning to get restless?"

"Shall I drop him with me cosh?"

"Not for the moment. There, brother, just as I said. You've antagonized him. Last man that did that spent more than a month in hospital."

"From the little I can see of his face I'd say I had nothing to do with his feelings. He wouldn't understand words of more than one syllable."

"Keep your remarks until afterwards. Maybe you won't feel like making them then. Sam's quite an artist. Takes a personal pride in making a good job of things. Never likes to kill because it causes such a stir. If you say much more maybe he'll risk the stir."

"An intentional pun?" asked Verrell. He sighed. "I thought not — be too much to ask." As he spoke he studied the distance between himself and the man with the gun. It had been judged nicely. Too far for him to jump forward. Near enough to ensure that 'Susie' would hit him, even allowing for the average inaccuracy of a revolver-shot.

"Better laugh while you can. Got a safe?"

"If I had it would be completely empty."

'Susie' looked at his watch. "We'll find it. Turn round and face the wall."

Verrell hesitated.

"If you want lead in your liver, stay put. I'm easy."

He thought the last sentence was probably only too accurate. He turned and faced the wall.

"Put your hands up over your head. If you don't know how, think of the films."

A snort of laughter recorded the fact that Sam had at last found something he could understand.

"Shut up. Get in and give him the treatment. The longer he's out the better."

The floor creaked slowly as the man moved forward.

Verrell waited, poised, every muscle tense. He counted four strides then felt the man behind him. His ears caught the faint hiss of hurried breathing, the rustle of clothes as an arm was raised. Mentally he followed the arm up in the air until it was at the limit of its backward stretch. Then he moved. With bewildering speed. He jumped up, thrust his feet against the wall and pushed backwards with all his strength, crunched into the body of the man behind.

Sam was caught off balance. He staggered away, trying to draw some air into his bruised lungs. Verrell half twisted as he fell, landed on hands and knees, threw himself forward in a somersault. 'Susie' fired. The bullet gouged the air a bare inch above the twisting body and slammed into the wall.

Then Verrell gripped the arm holding the gun and with every ounce of strength forced it upwards. The thug bellowed with rage, tried to shake himself free. The two bodies closed together and Verrell completed the arm-lock. A quick twist of his own arms, and the gun was dropped with a squeal of pain. He kicked it away, released his hold and swayed sideways. The cosh swept down from behind and missed him by scant inches. For a split second Sam was off balance as he leaned forward from the momentum of the missed stroke. Verrell slammed his foot up and pushed. There was a grunt, a thud. A table skidded backwards, taking Sam with it.

Verrell turned and saw 'Susie' was half-way to the fallen gun. He leapt forward and wrapped his arms round the other's neck, then twisted. It was a killing hold. Before Sam could rise to his feet, his companion had slumped to the ground, unconscious.

"Quite a party!" said Verrell pleasantly. "I take it you'll stay to the end?"

The other hunched his shoulders. He dropped the cosh, pulled a knife out of his pocket. A thin blade shot forward out of the sheath as he pressed a small button.

Verrell watched Sam slide forward on the balls of his feet, keeping both hands in front of him and near together. The stance of a man who knew how to use a knife.

They came together. Sam lunged with his right hand in a feint, whipped the knife across to his left and slashed downwards in a disembowelling action. Verrell swayed backwards, chopped down with the edge of his hand on the others neck.

"Why the change? Feel you can do more damage with a knife?"

Sam tried a straight downward hack. Verrell caught the blow with one hand just below the knife. He whipped his other hand round and back until he could grip his own wrist. He jerked backwards. The bone cracked. Sam squealed with pain.

"Effective — but regrettably painful."

A smashing left to the nose filled Sam's eyes with streams of burning tears. A right to the chin hurled him backwards. When he hit the ground he lay there.

Verrell eased his shoulders. He straightened his tie and collar before he crossed into the next room. At the bottom of a cupboard was a coil of thin, but strong, rope. He took it into the other room together with two kitchen chairs.

"Get up and sit down here."

Sam staggered to his feet and did as he was bid.

"Put your arms down the side here." Working quickly Verrell lashed the other securely to the chair, at the same time tying the bonds so that they provided a rough sling for the broken arm.

He picked 'Susie' up and sat him down in the other chair. Half-way through lashing him to the chair he paused for a brief moment. When he resumed he was less careful about making certain the rope was tight.

The task completed, he picked up the revolver from the floor, crossed to the cocktail-cabinet and poured out a drink.

"Cheers."

Sam stared at him, face contorted with fear and pain. The scarves of both men had fallen from their faces. They made a good pair. One smooth, thin-lipped, vicious. The other heavy, brutal.

Verrell lit a cigarette. A new uproar about the evils of smoking was getting under way. It was just too bad. Right then he wanted one, whether it gave him curling toe-nails or not.

'Susie' mumbled something, jerked at his bonds. Then he regained full consciousness. He ceased struggling, stared at Verrell defiantly.

"Good! Glad you've come round. One or two questions I want to ask you." He exhaled slowly.

Chapter Five

The silence in the room was deep.

"What's going to happen to us?" Sam could stand the tension no longer.

"Pipe down." 'Susie' grimaced as the sound of his own voice tore at his aching head.

"How many scenes does your big strong hero act have?" asked Verrell gently.

"Cut it out, brother."

"I didn't have time to mention it before, but I object to being called brother by something of your description."

"Never mind what..." He tailed off uneasily. The look the other gave him could have meant many things, none of which was pleasant.

"What's your name?" Verrell ripped out, addressing the big man.

"Sam Tr "

"I said to stow it."

Verrell chuckled. "Glad to see you conform to precedent. Having done so, now forget the histrionics of your friend and finish what you were going to say."

"He isn't saying any more."

"Are you posing as an authority?"

"Listen, mug. If you don't want to end up on a slab of marble you'll let us go."

Verrell finished his drink. "Nice to see such spirit. Hope you still have it at the end of your ten years breaking up stones. Or is that too cruel an occupation for these days?"

"I'm warning you." His warning might have carried weight were it not all too obvious that had his knees not been lashed to the chair they would have been knocking together.

"I don't find the prospect as alarming as you obviously think I should. I tied those knots securely."

"Start smiling when the rest of the boys catch up with you."

"The rest?" Verrell showed some interest.

"I said three of us were necessary. Him and his ruddy talking." Sam spoke with feeling. He had collected a smashed arm which hurt like hell, a sufficient number and variety of bruises to ensure it would be days before he could sit, stand, or lie in comfort.

Verrell stubbed out his cigarette. "Perhaps four would have been safer."

"You wouldn't be so ruddy cocky now," snarled 'Susie'. "And you won't be so cocky next time."

"Will you still be after my silver ash-trays?"

"We was told to…" started Sam.

"We wasn't told to do anything."

There was another pause. Verrell regarded the two men impartially. "I've been meaning to compliment you on your team work. The 'phone call was well timed."

"Don't know what you're talking about."

He took no notice of 'Susie's' interruption. "You waited outside the flat, 'phoned your superior as soon as I returned. He very neatly distracted my attention."

"You like your voice, don't you, brother?"

For a brief second Verrell's languid attitude changed. The expression in his eyes hardened, and the two men saw the steel which lay beneath the velvet surface. "Don't say that again."

'Susie' licked his lips. He was horribly afraid.

"Why were you sent along to beat me up?"

"I don't know. Never ask questions."

"We'll try a little memory-reviving. Think it might be effective?"

'Susie* licked his lips again. "It won't do any good — threatening us."

"No?" Verrell's smile was mocking.

Sam moaned. His arm was sending tearing pains through his body and head. If that were not enough, it was quite obvious the smiling man they had come to beat up was enjoying himself. He had an idea that the harder he yelled, the more the other would smile.

"Well?" suggested Verrell.

'Susie' interrupted: "Shut your trap, Sam, and keep it shut."

"Who sent you, and why?"

"I "

"You heard what I said," snapped 'Susie'.

Sam looked uncertain, but evidently his companion's threat was very real. "Go chase yourself," he told Verrell in a thick mutter.

"As you wish. Before we start I'll have another drink." He walked across to the cocktail-cabinet and slowly helped himself to a drink. He was working on their nerves, and unless his sense of timing was wrong it was the moment to disappear.

"To the successful conclusion of our little enterprise," he toasted.

"You fool." 'Susie' twisted in his chair. "What the hell do you think the coppers'll say when they hear what you've done? You'll be in along with us. We'll get you for a squealer."

Verrell smiled pleasantly. "Naturally, I shall deny everything. Now, if you'll excuse me I must away and get things ready. Won't keep you long."

He moved into the bedroom, crossed to the window and opened it. One of the unorthodox charms of his flat was that a convenient drain-pipe led straight down into the tiny courtyard. It gave him a second exit from his flat.

Rapidly he shinned down the drain-pipe into the yard, crossed out into the street. If his guess were correct, somewhere in the immediate vicinity would be a car. He tried to his left but drew a blank. He turned, found what he was looking for forty yards up the street.

It was a good, solid, dependable English saloon car. He reckoned that when the two men finally reached it they would use every ounce of such speed as it possessed. Five minutes was sufficient to locate the necessary tool and loosen one of the wheel-nuts.

In the flat the two men could stand the silence no longer.

"Jim, what's he going to do?" Sam was not made in the mould of a martyr.

"Wait a bit longer and you'll find out." The other tried to put up a strong front, but his eyes betrayed him. "Why the hell didn't you use a knife on him?"

"I tried. That's how I got me arm broke! It hurts like hell."

"Good." Jim spat on the floor. "So much for all your talk. The bloke who could carve anyone up as neat as a whistle. What happens? The only one who gets carved up is you. And shut up howling about your arm — you're not the only one who's hurt. My neck ain't ever going to get straight again."

"You didn't do so good yourself!" Sam was stung to retort by the injustice of the other's words. "If you'd shot him we wouldn't be here now."

"Always belly-aching."

Conversation ceased by mutual agreement. Jim twisted in his chair. He flexed his arms and felt the rope give slightly. "Here, try your ropes. He may be ruddy clever, but he doesn't know much about tying knots." He instinctively lowered his voice.

41

"Try the ropes... with me arm bust?"

"Then shut up."

Jim squirmed his body round until he could obtain some leverage against the back of the chair with his shoulders. The bonds moved.

"Give me the tip if you hear him."

Sam nodded, his face alive with hope.

Jim's wrists were lashed together. He strained heavily, trying to force them apart. The effort caught him off balance, and together with the chair he fell sideways on to the floor. Sweating with fear he lay as he had fallen.

The silence continued, unnaturally. It seemed impossible that the noise had gone unheard. But as the seconds became minutes he took heart. He threshed around, jerking backwards and forwards. Suddenly one of the loops of rope slackened. Another pull and he had one hand loose.

Two minutes later he was standing, free.

"Give me a hand — quick," pleaded Sam.

Jim did as asked, while remaining ready at the slightest warning to leave his companion and save his own skin.

Behind the door Verrell listened intently. He had changed into a suit best described as shapeless, colourless, and smelly. On his head an equally repulsive hat drooped.

About to move, he remembered money. A few notes and a small pile of silver lay on the reading-table by his bed. He pocketed them. Another quick check at the door and then, by way of his private 'back door', he left the flat for the second time in twenty minutes.

Sam knew what would happen should Verrell return before he was freed. Consequently, his nerves played havoc with his system. It seemed to his disordered mind that Jim was taking twice as long as he need. He appealed for haste, was immediately told to keep quiet.

At last the rope fell at his feet and he was able to move. So great was his relief, he forgot the pain in his arm.

They left the flat with ludicrous haste. Jim was first on the pavement — he had two good elbows. He raced towards the car, and with a sob of thanks reached the driving-seat. By the time Sam reached the other door he had already started the engine.

"We'll get the swine for this," he snarled. He let the clutch out sharply, and the car jerked away from the pavement.

Verrell followed them — in a taxi. At the back of the flat was a rank where, even at that hour of the morning, there was always at least one cab, the driver of which would be in the small shelter dozing. There had been no trouble in borrowing the one cab he had found waiting; the lack of an ignition key he had overcome by joining two wires at the back of the dashboard.

He thought the two ahead of him would soon be in need of a taxi. He was right.

Jim came to a comer and swung hard over. The sudden twist was too much for the near-side front wheel. It came off and went spinning gaily down the road in front of the car. For a wild moment he thought he was seeing things — discovered he was not when the car tilted abruptly over to one side accompanied by the sound of grinding metal.

Sam was thrown sideways, and cracked his broken arm against the door. He yelped.

"The quicker we're out of this the better. He'll be along before we damn well know what's what. Of all the blasted times for this to happen... Hey, taxi!" Jim waved and whistled, trying to make certain the driver did not go by.

Verrell tried not to stop too promptly.

They clambered inside.

"Forty-nine, Clements Road, and get a move on. Back of Hammersmith Broadway."

Verrell drove off.

"What are you going to do about the car?" Sam groaned.

"Nothing. One of the boys whizzed it earlier on. Got a fag?"

"Here."

"Thanks."

They lit up. There was silence as the car drove along the deserted roads.

Verrell took his time, still uncertain as to his next move.

Sam was the first to speak. He had been thinking. An unusual occupation. "What's he going to say?"

Jim shifted uneasily. It was a case of great minds thinking alike. The same problem had occurred to him. He had been wondering if the best solution would not be to vanish. "We'll tell him this bloke was entertaining," he suggested at last. "We can say we hung around for a bit, but didn't get a chance to beat him up."

Sam rose to unsuspected heights of intelligence. "You told him Verrell was alone when 3/ou rung. And what about me busted arm?"

"Why the hell didn't I keep my blasted mouth shut? Not much good saying anything now you've gone and made a fool of yourself. By rights it ought to be his neck, not your arm."

"You ain't the only one who thinks that."

Jim returned to the advisability of not reporting. It would mean the loss of much money. Against that he might manage to stay alive. But would…? His mind was made up for him. By sheer luck Verrell had found the address.

The two passengers stepped out. Tim fumbled in his pocket. "How much?"

Verrell turned to look at the meter, noticed with a sinking feeling that he had forgotten to start it.

The other was not slow to notice the fact. "Brother, you've chosen the wrong bloke to try that chestnut on. I was weaned on taxis which tried a quick crook."

"Sorry, mate," mumbled Verrell. "Don't rightly know what happened."

"Not much you don't! Next time try it out on someone what ain't got all his wits about him." He was too proud of his own eloquence to notice anything strange in the episode. "Here's eight bob for the two of us. If you don't like it, go whistle."

Jim watched the taxi drive away. "Blasted crook," he snapped.

Together they entered the house.

Verrell returned the car to the rank from which he had taken it. He pinned a couple of notes to the upholstery as recompense for the driver; as an afterthought he also left the fare he had just received.

He returned to his flat and thankfully changed out of the smelly clothing. He was in two minds as to whether he should investigate the house in Hammersmith. It would be fast approaching daylight by the time he got there. He grinned. There was nothing to lose, and should everyone have gone to bed he could have a quick look round.

He crossed to the wardrobe in his bedroom, pressed a hidden switch which released a panel at the back. In the small space revealed were the clothes he wore as Blackshirt.

He had two cars. His second was used when he wanted to be inconspicuous. For a long time he had kept an old saloon in a garage in a dead-end road that was well off the beaten track. Recently, however, he had been forced to find both a new garage and another car. A long search had been rewarded by a lock-up garage in a small mews, in which he kept a car as undistinguished as the first.

Briskly he walked along the pavements in the direction of the mews. A white scarf was folded carefully round his neck and tucked inside his evening coat. He looked as though he were returning from a good night out.

The house was semi-detached, typical of the suburbs. A miniature garden fronted it, had received no attention for many months. To the right and left were similar buildings.

Blackshirt paused to make certain the street was empty, then stepped inside the gate and under the slight protection of a young tree. He took off the white scarf, adjusted the hood, put on the gloves. Without a vestige of white about him, he became a pool of darkness, invisible unless a beam of light fell directly on him.

To the right of the house was a door giving access to the back. It was locked. He took out a small bunch of skeleton-keys. The third one worked. He opened the door and passed through into the back garden. A misnomer, since it was in even worse condition than the front.

Two doors led into the house. To judge from the stone step and nearby dustbin the first opened into the kitchen. The other was more elaborate, half glass. He adjusted the shutter on his torch, then switched it on. The pinhead of light passed over the lock of the first door. Thirty seconds later he slowly turned the handle and eased the door open.

The kitchen was like the garden, in a mess. The table was littered with empty tins and the remains of several meals. The sink did work normally undertaken by a dustbin; the floor was covered with scraps of food, cigarette-butts, and an overriding layer of dirt. Empty beer-bottles lay everywhere.

At the far end of the kitchen was a half-open glass door, and beyond, a short passage leading into the hall. To the right a flight of stairs curved upwards. As he drew level with the bottom stair he heard the hum of voices from above.

He mounted the flight, stair by stair, taking care as he did so not to transfer the balance of his weight until he could feel fairly certain that the boards would not creak.

From a sharp half-turn to the right he reached the upper landing, at the far end of which was a thin line of light coming from under a door. Like the stairs, the passage was uncarpeted, so each step had to be taken at a snail's pace. At last he was near enough to distinguish what was being said.

"Shove that bottle over, mate."

"Keep your shirt on — it's coming." Jim's voice was unmistakable.

"And see something's left in it."

"Go chase yourself, brother."

"Shut up, both of you." It was a new speaker.

Outside Blackshirt recognized the voice, identified it as the man who had earlier obtained a 'wrong number' on the telephone.

"I'll shut up when it suits me."

"You'll do it here and now. Stop thinking you're so mighty important, Jim. Another mistake from you and you won't even be able to cry Uncle."

"All I said was "

"The Boss was not quite certain what to do with you." The speaker paused to let the warning sink in. "Having sorted that one out maybe we can get to bed. Damn near time for breakfast."

"We ain't finished the bottle yet. Plenty of time to get some sleep. We're not moving before afternoon, are we?"

"Not unless we hear some more. Shove that bottle over, I can do with a last one before bed. You blokes certain you know what's got to be done?"

They grunted.

"Sam was fool enough to break his arm, so you, Mac, take over his part. The rest of us carry on as we were. And if there's a slip up with this, God help the man responsible! Got that, Jim?"

"How many more ruddy times do I have to tell you it wasn't my fault? How was I to know the swine?"

A sarcastic laugh interrupted the speaker. "Of course it wasn't your fault. You only had a gun, Sam only had a cosh and a knife. Odds were too even!"

"I said shut up, Mac. They made a mess of things, but they aren't the first."

"When I get my hands on him," snarled Jim, "there won't be any more of his funny stuff. I'll croak him sure as my name's Longton. If the swine had only fought properly…"

Blackshirt chuckled. He liked the sporting spirit.

"Got a fag on you, Parson?"

"Take the packet. One of these days you'll buy your own!"

A pause as all three men helped themselves.

"Here's a light," said Parson. "One last item you'd better drive into those thick skulls of yours. Not a thing is to be left around here when we move. No scraps of paper."

"You're giving a lot of orders."

"Objecting?"

"Well, it's only that I think "

"Try and get one thing straight in that small mind of yours. You're paid to do, not think. When the boss is away, I tell you what to do. And don't forget that you aren't as popular as you might be." He spoke loudly.

Blackshirt eased a foot which was trying to go numb.

"One more thing. Sam was going to drive that car you smashed up between you. I want another one in the morning. Make sure it's a fast one."

"You said we wouldn't be moving before afternoon."

Parson sighed. "Stop doing my job for me. We aren't going anywhere until then. But how are we supposed to get down to Hampshire? By rocket?"

"Always something," grumbled Mac. "I'm going to get some doss. Finish that drink up, Jim, and come on. Do without you waking me up just as I get to sleep."

Blackshirt turned the handle of the door with care, opened it until he could see through the space between it and the doorpost.

Only two men were in sight. One was Jim; he judged the other to be Mac. He was more interested in the third member.

Satisfied that none of the men was paying any attention to the door he continued to move it, a fraction of an inch at a time, until he could see all three.

Parson was dressed in a sober suit, had a white shirt and quiet tie. His face was remarkably young-looking. But for one thing he might have appeared as respectable and ordinary as other men in London who dressed somewhat formally. The lie to such a picture was given by his eyes. They were cold and calculating, with eyelids that gave an impression of hoods.

Blackshirt felt the door touch something. He checked his 50

weight, ready to move away at speed. There was a faint movement which drew the attention of the men in the room. One of the bottles lying around the floor hesitated, then rolled a few inches.

"I thought there was a filthy draught round my feet. Can't you ever shut a door?"

Jim jumped to his feet, face creased in ugly lines. 'Too right I can. And did."

Blackshirt stepped back. He had his torch in his hand and switched it on. The tiny beam showed an electric-light bulb, unshaded, to the right of his head. He twisted it out of its socket.

Jim pulled the door wide open and stepped out. "If anyone's thinking of mucking around here he won't get far." He peered along the shaft of light streaming from the room behind.

"You've got the jumps. No one's there." Mac was alongside him. "Still, now we've moved, it's bed for me." He yawned. "Smoked too many fags — mouth tastes like a slice of rubber."

Jim crossed to a switch, pressed it down. "What's going on round here? This light was all right when I came up."

"Probably got the wrong switch. It's the top one," snapped Parson. "Let me do it." He pushed his way across.

Blackshirt moved with speed. One moment he had been hidden in the gloom to the side of the door, nothing but a blob of blackness — the next he had whipped the door shut, cutting off the light.

"Open the door. Who shut it? Blast this switch!" Parson snapped it up and down.

Mac turned and placed his hand on the door-handle. An arm encircled his neck and pressed. "Keep quiet, brother." It was a perfect imitation of Jim's voice. "Just something to teach you to take more care when you speak to me." A knee was placed in the small of his back, the pressure round his neck increased. In a wild flurry of arms and legs he crashed to the ground.

"What the hell's going on between you two?" snapped Parson.

Mac swore profusely. "I'll rip you up for that." He lunged forward and caught someone's head a crack with his knuckles.

Jim yelled. "Lay off it. That hurt/'

"You surprise me! Next time swipe someone smaller than yourself."

"I didn't flaming well touch you."

"Someone did. And it was you yelling down my ear."

"Like hell it was."

"Parson, you heard him. Now the liar's trying to say he didn't..." He ended in a frantic yell. Blackshirt, enjoying himself immensely, had stamped heavily on his foot.

"Stop it, you fools," snapped Parson. "Open that door so I can see."

Blackshirt waited until Mac reached the handle of the door, then repeated the first performance, even down to the same little speech. It produced chaos. The unfortunate man picked himself up from the floor and gave vent to his feelings both in words and action. A flood of strong English was punctuated by whirlwind motions with his hands. Twice he thumped Jim in the face.

Parson gave up his futile efforts to make the landing light work and took two steps forward. He called out to the others to pack up the row. It was then that he was gripped by the back of his collar and spun round sideways with much power. He threshed forward into a tangle of legs, cannoned off into the wall.

"I'll break every blasted bone in your bodies," he stormed, savagely rubbing his head.

He stood up. He was turned round and again propelled forcibly forward. This time he brought the other two down with him, and in resentful mood slammed out with fists and feet.

Blackshirt thought it was time he left. Very soon one of the yelling combatants might remember to strike a match. Silently he reached the head of the stairs, then made his way down. At the bottom he paused. From above came many sounds. The battle was not yet over.

Chapter Six

Verrell was up late the next morning. Late even by his standards, which were as elastic as any author's. By the time he had dressed and shaved it was well after ten.

"Good morning, sir." Roberts greeted him as unemotionally as always. "Shall I get breakfast, sir?"

"Thanks. Don't worry beyond toast and coffee."

"Very good, sir. I've placed the papers on the table."

Verrell sat down and skimmed through the news. There was little of interest. The mystery of the theft from the Freshman collection was past history. Another theft of bank-notes from a mail-bag had taken its place.

He put the paper aside as his valet brought in breakfast. Afterwards he enjoyed his first cigarette of the day, then settled down to work.

By six that evening he had made good progress. Sufficiently good to warrant his ceasing work and taking a brisk walk to clear his head. On the way back, after a distance which would have been considered fantastic by most Londoners, he bought an evening paper. This one contained something which did interest him. Very much so. It was a small paragraph in the stop-press column, necessarily vague and incomplete, but undoubtedly absorbing. There had been a burglary that afternoon in a house near Lymington, Hampshire. The thieves had been disturbed by the owner, whom they had brutally attacked before leaving with many valuable objects; in addition, they took two paintings by Old Masters.

The identity of the thieves was obvious. Parson and company had struck quickly and savagely. Their object, ostensibly, whatever they could find. In fact, there could have been only one objective. A painting by Bassete...

With rising excitement he realized his original guess had been correct. Or at the very least the odds were shortening. In some manner the paintings were the clue to the hiding-place of von Steiner's looted wealth.

If that were true something else became self-evident. The painting which had been stolen from the Freshman collection had not supplied the answer. Possibly the answer lay between the five. There might yet be time for him to take a hand in the game.

He renewed the walk with added zest. The General had owned five Bassete paintings. Two of them had already been stolen. Three remained.

He must find out where. He tried to think of someone who could tell him. Sir Edward might know. A telephone call soon dashed that hope. He was away for a day or two on business and Miss Diana was also out.

Walking away from the telephone he had a brainwave. He had forgotten John Tankerton, a member of his club, who painted the kind of nightmare beloved of 'advanced' circles.

Verrell reached the cocktail-bar of his club and grinned. Tankerton was there, indulging in his passion for pink gins. He was seated on a high stool talking rapidly to an acquaintance on his left. Verrell sat down on the stool on his right.

The bartender came across from the far end of the bar. "Good evening, sir. Nice to see you back. What would you like?"

"A John Collins, please."

At the sound of the new voice Tankerton broke off in the middle of a sentence and swung round.

"Verrell, by all that's holy! Haven't seen you in a month of Sundays. Name your poison."

"I've just ordered, thanks. Have one with me."

"Later — evening's young yet. How's the world of that prostituted art you call writing these days? Still turning out the same old theme?" He did not wait for an answer. "Time you chappies realized there's a resurrection in the Arts. Give the public something to chew on instead of pandering to them. They want their sluggish minds whipped up, not satiated by boy-meets-girl sob-stuff."

Verrell laughed. "You think we ought to write something nobody could read?"

"Sir, you mock me!" Despite the relatively early hour, he had already had a sufficient number of drinks to imagine he was an interesting speaker.

The man on the left of the artist seized the opportunity with commendable haste. He mumbled something, departed.

"If my writing followed your paintings I should have to include a translation with every book."

Tankerton vigorously finished the glass in front of him.

He signalled to the bartender and indicated both himself and Verrell.

"Listen to me." He dug his pointed finger into Verrell's shoulder. "Your true artist is the one who delves into new realms. He's not the one who treads the well-worn paths. That's the copyist. The man without intelligence. Could Dickens write? Certainly not! He merely carried on where Scott left off. Did he portray a new matter? No. Those scenes of London — dozens of other books have them. What did he have then, that the multitude should bow and praise him?"

Verrell made no attempt to answer this question. It was as well. He might not have been able to stop himself laughing.

"I'll tell you. He had popular acclaim based on the taste of the masses. His novels appealed to their senses because they were simple nonsense. Now, he might have been great. And I'll tell you how. If he had left this pattern of plot and character, and gone forward where there is no such artificial distinction. Another gin," he ended abruptly.

Verrell smiled politely. Sadly he reflected that if he did obtain the information he was seeking, it would be well earned.

Three pink gins later Tankerton was talking about Old Masters.

"Paint. Of course they could paint. So can a child of two. Call it good painting and you show your ignorance. What did they do? They painted what they actually saw!"

It was perfectly clear that this was the ultimate in decadence.

"And not only that, they thought they were artists when they did so. They didn't stop to realize that the artist had been submerged, lost. Look at it this way. Is he, or is he not, an individual with a mind of his own? Is he...?" It was good, solid, jargon which the speaker understood perfectly. Thereby being in a happier position than his listener.

It took another gin to reach Van Dyck.

"Good! There you go, aping the cry of others. You throw your hands in the air; sigh; exclaim. How exquisite the detail, how brilliant the faces, what character! Damn it, man, it's nothing but the work of a copyist. And what's more, he's been copied. So damn well all these snooty art critics couldn't tell the difference. Chap called Bassete took them all by their noses."

"I've heard about him."

'The man's showing signs of an inferior education." He called for another gin by way of celebration. It was a long time since anyone had listened to his views so patiently.

Verrell's patience was stretched to its limits when he finally reached the information he'd been seeking.

"Yes, there's one on view somewhere round here. Bought just after the experts decided they'd been had for suckers."

"Who bought it?"

"Someone with a sense of humour. That's who! Someone who knew precisely what an art critic's worth."

"You don't know who actually did get it?"

"No. And what's more... Hang on a tick. Blessed if one of the galleries didn't shake the world by buying and exhibiting it. Slap up against the genuine article."

"Where?"

"Where? Need you ask? Where could it be, but one of these places dedicated to a dead and best-forgotten art. Went through once and had to come out half-way to be ill."

"Do you mean it exhibits some of the old paintings?" hazarded Verrell.

Tankerton snorted. "The man's an idiot. Of course that's what I mean."

"What's the name of the Gallery?"

"How should I know? Ask someone who revels in such things. It's somewhere at the back of Oxford Street. The... the Gallery of Old Masters. That's it. Gallery of Old Frauds!"

In decency, Verrell should have stayed longer.

But Tankerton was... Tankerton!

The next morning Verrell visited the Gallery which had on exhibition the Bassete painting from the von Steiner collection. The building was a good solid piece of Victorian vandalism. There were many columns outside, much odd and disconcerting decorative plaster-work in the inside. It stood on its own, bounded on four sides by roads, a bulwark against encroaching modernity.

Despite its lack of architectural charm, the building housed 56

many fine works. Verrell passed through the various schools of painters, until he came to two Van Dycks... and the Basset e.

It was a wonderful forgery. Change the labels round, and not one person in a hundred thousand would have known. It was all most amusing. Except for one thing. That the authorities had bothered to include a painting worth pounds in a collection worth a few million.

There were few people around, and it was not difficult to start a conversation with one of the uniformed attendants.

Verrell indicated the Bassete painting. "Strange to find that here."

"I suppose it is, sir. Only fake in the whole exhibition. Fact is, sir, I think they put it in just to show how good a painter the other fellow was. Strikes me, if a man can do a job so well practically no one can tell it isn't an original, then I says he's a good painter."

He wondered how Tankerton would react to such a pronouncement. "Something in what you say," he agreed. "Has the collection been here long?"

"Best part of eighty years, sir. Man called Johnson started it. When he died he left it to the nation. It's been growing ever since."

"Must take some looking after?"

The man took off his cap and ran his hand over his forehead. "Takes more than a little, sir. Everything has to be just right. Apart from anything else there's an air-conditioning plant what was put in three years back. Cost a fortune, so I heard."

"Ever get anyone along who wants to poke an umbrella into one of the pictures?"

The man chuckled. "Not yet, sir. Nearest to that was one old dear who complained about the nudes. Though what I was supposed to do about it I don't know. Paint some clothes on, I suppose."

Verrell dutifully laughed. "How long are you kept patrolling?"

"Eight to six. The blokes on night-duty have to do the rest of the time; we do turn and turn about."

"You keep the place guarded at night-time, then?"

"Of course, sir. Never know when there might be a fire. What that would mean here ain't nobody's business. Patrol has to be on the move all night."

"You don't want anything stolen, either."

The man chuckled. "Don't have to worry about that end of things. The whole building is wired to an alarm that goes off in the police-station across the road as well as here. Some of those coppers can run! Remember once, my mate Bert wanted to go out and telephone his wife who wasn't too well at the time. He walked out of the side door without switching off the alarm. Next moment the place was knee-deep in uniforms. Poor old Bert, he felt no end of a fool."

Verrell looked at his watch. "Heavens, had no idea it was so late! I must shoot. Hope you don't go making any 'phone calls without doing the necessary."

"Not likely, sir. Not after the blasting Bert got from everyone. As he said afterwards, since his wife was right as rain by the time he got through, the call was wasted anyway."

Verrell left and strolled round the square formed by the Gallery. He was interested in the buildings which faced it. Two sides of the square were filled with shops, and in one corner of the second was the police-station. The other two were composed of large blocks of old buildings which had at one time been private houses, but were now offices.

As he walked along the fourth and last side of the square he came to the side door of the Gallery. It was in strict contrast to the impressive main entrance. A small door, perfectly plain in itself, which had not, however, escaped completely since it had a wholly unnecessary flat, out-jutting porch.

He returned slowly to his flat, pondering on what he had just seen. The nearness of the police-station was an immediate and pressing danger. Rather like the steel shutters of the Freshman collection.

As the simile came to mind he smiled slowly. A suspicion of excitement rose within him. Ostensibly it was a hurdle. But with a little adroit manoeuvring it might prove an easy one.

He reached his sitting-room and sat down, cast his mind back to what he had seen. Most punters would have thought the odds grim. But that was the way he had always liked them. First, if he were to overcome them, he must return to the Gallery with a camera. Measurements were essential.

He made his second visit after a good lunch, somewhat 58

spoiled by his preoccupation with the task before him. He used a self-developing camera and exposed an entire roll of films with shots from different angles. Then he measured the length of a shadow thrown by a post his own height, finally took a quiet and leisurely walk past the door, which enabled him to note how exposed it was to the view of passers-by. Satisfied there was nothing more to be done, he returned to his flat and studied the photos. A quick calculation was sufficient. The safety-factor was low enough to give a life insurance agent blood-pressure. But it was there.

He lit a last cigarette and lazily blew a smoke ring towards the ceiling. All that was needed to make the evening perfect was to find Parson and friends also making an attempt to obtain the picture. He felt, however, that it was asking too much.

He stubbed the cigarette out and stood up. Happy to pit his wits against the police, excited at the prospect of danger. Two factors which made him continue his double life long after it was no longer necessary to steal merely to live.

He walked blithely along a pavement that was empty of all but those whose job it was to be out at such times; or those, apparently like himself, returning from a night out. A patrolling constable wished him good evening and continued on his beat. Never realizing he had just spoken to the man whose capture would have ensured his quick promotion.

He reached the monstrous building which, in the subdued artificial light of the street-lamps, took on a faintly romantic air. He passed the police-station, came alongside the side door, paused to make certain he was unobserved while he drew on his gloves. With an agile jump he caught hold of the edge of the roof of the porch and pulled himself up. His calculations had been correct. There was room.

He adjusted his hood and was about to jump down when a car came in sight, drove round the square and away. For a short while he remained motionless. Judging everything to be quiet once more, he dropped to the ground and pulled a thin strip of celluloid out of his pocket. A quick movement of his wrist, and the Yale lock turned; the door clicked open. He slammed it shut again, jumped up and reached the ledge above the door.

Alarm bells rang inside the building. They rang in the police-station and echoed across the road. Though slightly muffled they still had sufficient force left to show that those inside the station must have received an awful blast to shake them out of their 'graveyard' watch. This was confirmed immediately. From the door under the illuminated blue lamp policemen dashed across the road, in one case minus tunic or helmet.

"Get those entrances covered," shouted a sergeant at the top of his voice. "Higgins, Fenton, stand by with me to go inside. Bellows, wait out here for the inspector. If you see a patrol car stop it, and get the men to give a hand."

The police raced to their appointed positions.

"You lads follow me inside," continued the sergeant. "Blow your whistles as soon as you see him. None of this fancy stuff of doing everything by yourself."

He dashed inside, contacted the watchmen immediately.

"Know where the entry's been made?"

"Not yet. Just about to start looking," replied the foremost of the two guards.

"Don't be in too much of a hurry!"

A patrol car drew up outside, directed there by wireless. The driver stood by; the other two occupants went inside.

An inspector, still half-asleep, arrived. He rubbed his eyes as though it would help him to wake more fully, cursed everybody and everything with fine impartiality. He met the constable's information with a grunt, pushed his way into the building.

"What's been touched?" he yelled across a room as he caught sight of the sergeant.

"Can't find anything as yet, sir."

"Dammit, have you looked? What about the windows and doors — anything opened or tampered with?"

"As far as I've checked, sir, nothing's been touched." He moved across to his superior.

"As far as you've checked! Has anything been tampered with?"

"No, sir. That is, I don't think so. But the alarm went off."

The inspector loudly cursed life for having given him such 60 idiots to work with. The sergeant did the same, under his breath.

The search continued and drew a blank.

"Man must have been scared off," said the inspector. "Or else it was one of you two 'phoning his wife again?" He glared at the guards.

They returned the stare with interest, and said 'No' in six rude ways.

The inspector made a 'huh'-ing sound. He ordered one last check throughout the building, then led his forces out and away. Peace returned.

As the police-car left, and the last constable filed back into the police-station, Blackshirt stretched out and let his legs dangle over the side. It was sheer bliss, after the long time he had lain cramped, unable to move. Gradually his muscles eased themselves and he was ready for the next move. He dropped to the ground, took out the piece of celluloid, and repeated his performance. Practice making perfect, it enabled him to reach the top of the porch even quicker than before.

The sergeant had got his boots off when the alarm clanged for the second time. He had a corn which needed attention. Was about to attend with a penknife when the hideous row started again. He involuntarily sliced downwards. He swore, hobbled into his boots, formed the rearguard of the file of policemen returning to the Old Masters' Gallery.

He ordered two of his men to follow him, marched down the short corridor and met the two guards coming out of the small room which was their headquarters for the night.

"Your perishing alarm rang again," he snapped.

"No!... I thought it was the fairies singing."

"Fairies! You'll get fairies, chum!"

"Change the record, mate."

"If we don't find something this time I'll have a few words to say in the morning. Be the last time you try making fools of the police."

Nevertheless, even as he swopped pleasantries, the sergeant was organizing the men for the second search of the building.

There was one very large central room, off which smaller rooms opened. To pass from one to another of the latter one had to go through the former. One constable was stationed in the centre of the large room, while the others covered the remaining galleries. In less than ten minutes they were all back together again.

"It ain't April the first," remarked the sergeant heavily.

"Well I'm blowed, and here was I thinking it was." The smaller of the two guards refused to be abashed by the surplus of uniforms. "Never mind, it's the funniest sight I've seen for years!"

"Laugh some more tomorrow. When you both goes down on the charge sheet."

"Here — easy on!" The joke — always assuming there were one — appeared to be getting out of hand. "How should I know what's happening?"

"How? That's a good one! You're the only ones in this flaming building. You tell us why we have to jump up and down like a pack of cards."

"It's what you're paid to do. Public servants, aren't you?"

"Public what?" yelled the sergeant. "Coming from the likes of you!"

Relations became even more strained before the police finally retired.

The sergeant managed to get the final word. "If it goes again I hopes you like it. Tell me if you gets your throats cut!"

Back at the station he sat down, wearily took off his boots, and called for some tea. He sighed. Not so long to go before he could retire on a modest pension. That day couldn't come too soon. After many years at the job he saw in it nothing but grinding monotony. This view was confirmed in a peremptory fashion. The alarm bells clanged again. He spilt some of the tea on to his uniform.

"Higgins!" he shouted at the top of his voice.

The constable appeared.

"Go over and tell those humorists that if this ruddy bell goes again I'll clap them in gaol for the night. And if they still say they don't know anything about it, they'll stay in the cells all tomorrow as well."

"Very good, Sergeant. Seems a proper mix-up."

"You get along and do as you're told, me lad. Never mind the pow-wow."

The constable walked across the road.

Blackshirt was examining the Bassete painting. He had passed the guards while they were still swearing at the alarm.

There was enough light for him to dispense with his torch. He checked the front of the frame, took it down and examined the back. The cursory examination was not enough to show him what he had hoped to find. He took from the inside of his coat a large square of brown paper and some string, quickly made a parcel of the painting. Ready to leave, he paused, listening to the murmur of voices from the guards' room.

There was a movement, then the solid sound of regulation boots on the stone flooring.

"You tell that to your sergeant."

"Not me, chum. Got a wife and two kids to support." The constable left to report back to the station.

Blackshirt followed him at a discreet distance. With one smooth motion he was past the room in which the smaller guard was still telling his companion what he thought of the police force. He paused at the outside door and looked at the switch. He grinned. Why turn it off? He undid the lock, went out, closed the door behind him.

No one ever recorded what the harassed police said when the alarm went for the fourth time that night.

Chapter Seven

Blackshirt reached his flat and poured out a drink. He was feeling the effects of two nights with a minimum of sleep, but there was one thing to be done before he could rest. To examine the painting more closely. He unwrapped it and laid it on the table. A careful examination disclosed nothing. He took out a bag of tools from a drawer and chose a screwdriver. Even though he knew the painting was a fake he suffered the pangs of vandalism as he took the frame to pieces ready, if necessary, to rip the actual canvas. It was not. In a corner of the frame he came across a small space hollowed out. Inside was a roll of thin tissue-paper.

"Well, I'm damned!" he muttered delightedly. "Struck oil first time. That'll make the others curl their beards."

His enjoyment was short-lived. He unrolled the paper; it was roughly 42" x 15", and had on it only two large numbers. Nothing else. The upper corners were missing.

He stared at it with something approaching dislike. He had gone to a lot of trouble to obtain the painting. It might not be in order for him to say so... but the theft had been cleverly planned and executed. His efforts deserved greater success than they appeared to have achieved.

The numbers — a five and a two — probably meant something. On the other hand, in his present state of mind, he was prepared to believe they were an advertisement for Heinz products. Fifty-two. So very helpful!

He finished the drink and considered the situation. He was faced with two possibilities. First, he had the solution in front of him. Secondly, he only had part of it — presumably a fifth. He had miscounted, as he immediately realized. There was a third possibility. That what he had was nothing.

The missing corners might be suggestive. What, if anything, they suggested was another matter.

Tired as he was, he determined to do one more thing before going to bed. He lit a gas-ring in the kitchen and held the paper to the heat. The result was completely negative.

By lunch-time the next day Verrell was consigning von Steiner to many places. Puzzle as he might he could not reach any feasible explanation of the meaning of the paper, or of the numbers on it. Did they even mean anything? He did not know. But there was one way to find out. If he could track down another von Steiner Bassete, and compare the hidden paper — if there were one — he might start moving.

Diana Freshman was expected back at her home that afternoon. He would go down and see her. For one thing, he might be able to find out where the other paintings had gone; for another, he could look once more at the scene of the 'perfect' crime.

The drive was fast, since he met with little resistance from 64 would-be suicides in other vehicles. Diana made no secret of the fact that she was glad to see him.

"You're becoming something of a regular, Richard. Soon have to keep your place at the table always at the ready."

She smiled as she linked her arm in his and led the way into the house.

"Have you come to take me for a swim?"

"If you care to," he answered unabashed.

"Something tells me, Richard, your last reply was hardly truthful."

"Damned if you ever do believe me these days," he protested.

She laughed.

"Did you have a good time whilst you were away?" he asked.

She did not answer until they were in the small drawingroom.

"As good as one ever has on a duty visit. One of my aunts, quite ridiculously maiden, who still thinks a night-club is only patronized by the other type of woman. Still, I suppose she's quite a dear really."

"Which part of the country?"

"Just past Maidenhead, on the River Lodden. Never mind her — it's an odd time for coffee, but would you like some?"

He grinned. "Maybe it's odd, but I should."

She rang the bell, gave the order when the butler appeared, upset at having his afternoon disturbed.

"Anything fresh happened?" asked Verrell casually.

"In connection with what?" She was all innocence — -with a most becoming dimple.

"The little spot of trouble you had the other day."

She laughed happily. "Call it a little spot of trouble in father's presence and he'll forbid you ever to set foot in the house. The answer in one word is — nothing. Big men and little men have come along and scratched their heads, then gone away. I believe officially they're all working on promising leads. Actually we've still one constable left, but just what he's meant to be doing I don't think even he knows."

He stared into space. Small wonder the policemen were only 'working on promising leads'. Since no matter how much one wriggled round the question, the theft was impossible!

A man had entered. He could touch nothing without setting off an alarm. Three — or was it four? — minutes later the alarm went off. The shutters turned the room into a steel-lined vault. Guards outside testified the man had not returned past them.

The room was opened up. It was empty. The man had disappeared. So had a painting. The farthest point the man could have reached after the alarm went off, and before the shutters dropped, was well short of any point of exit. Through which he could not possibly have passed even had he reached it.

The theft that couldn't be, but was!

"Read any good books lately?"

Returning from his private world he realized Diana was smiling at him.

"I'm sorry, I "

"Undoubtedly. Richard, are you writing another book?"

"Trying to, though without much success at the moment. Just at one of those sticky patches where the words won't come." He thought it unnecessary to add that he had hardly given them a chance.

"Will you give me a copy when it comes out?"

"Good Heavens, no! You buy it from the local bookseller — create a demand."

She pouted. "That's mean of you. I've been doing some wonderful work on your behalf ever since I first met you. Telling all my friends they simply must read your books."

"My apologies. Didn't realize the good work going on around here."

They sat back and enjoyed the coffee poured out by Beach, who, silently, but with some force, managed to indicate his disapproval of the innovation.

"Diana, might I go along and have a look at the collection?"

"I was wondering how long it would be before you got around to asking. Thought you couldn't wait much longer!"

"By the way," he asked casually, "have you any idea of what happened to the other paintings?"

"Which ones?"

"The Bassetes. The General collected five of them."

She shrugged her shoulders. "Now you're asking! Frankly, 66 I don't take the interest in the things that father does. I remember his buying the one which we've had stolen, because he dragged me off to the auction. What interested me was the fabulous price he paid for it. Especially now I know it's worth so little. I could have worn Dior exclusives for years and years."

"Were the other four auctioned at the same time?"

"I don't think so. Just as well, if you stop to think about it. Father might have bought all five — then think what life would be like!"

"Pity. I was wondering what happened to the other four."

"Now you come to mention it, the Old Man was wondering the same thing."

Verrell looked a trifle blank.

"My father," she explained lightly. "One of the names he cannot bear. He's just had another of his great ideas. Wants to buy one of the other fakes and hang it in the space in the museum. He can still call it a Van Dyck and his pride will be mollified. He mumbled something about it the other day; said he'd get in touch with a firm which had sold one."

He looked up. "Did your father mention the name of the firm?"

"He did make some comment. Called them a pack of rogues. So far as I could gather they once charged him too much for a painting. Still, he bought it. Why all the sudden interest?"

"I was just wondering…"

"You think there's some connection between them — that's why one was stolen from us?"

He hedged. "In a way."

"Don't be in too much of a hurry to tell me! I wouldn't mind betting what's left in my bank account something pretty good is stewing in that head of yours."

He laughed lightly. "Anything is possible. Would you be remembering the name of the firm your father mentioned?"

"I would not be remembering. Not at the moment, anyway. It may come later, in which case I'll let you know. Free of charge, too."

Shortly after that, they made their way to the collection. Everything was as Verrell had last seen it. The space on the wall upset the careful planning of the other paintings. He walked across to speak to the lone constable personifying the tenacity of the police.

"Still at it?"

"One way of putting it, sir," he replied. He was fed up with facing culture day after day.

"Nothing turned up yet?"

"No more it will, sir. Whoever did this job took a course from the Houdini bloke."

"No secret passages?"

The constable sighed, obviously, but without force sufficient to make it rude. It correctly expressed his feelings. "No, sir," he admitted.

Verrell hesitated no longer, but left the poor man to his own devices. It was not fair to intrude on such despair.

"Has the master-mind deduced it was by a seven-foot pygmy with clean-shaven features and a beard?" Diana asked teasingly.

He chuckled. "You've tripped up somewhere. Seven-foot-one, judging by the invisible footstep."

They passed the guard outside the door and were halfway down the corridor when he halted. "Bear with me for a moment, will you? I want to look at something."

He walked to the end of the side passage where the guards' lockers were situated. Then he retraced his steps, half-running. He did the same thing walking. The result was what he had expected. The maximum time that the guard could have taken from the hook, where he kept his coat, to the main entrance before the swing doors, dovetailed with the rest of the facts.

"What has that proved?" she asked.

"Nothing — beyond the fact that it couldn't be."

Johns, the guard, walked across. " 'Afternoon, sir. Seeing what it was like?"

"Trying to. You must be fed up with the whole business by now?"

"You're right there, sir. It isn't only the police. It's the people who come along to see the collection. At least, that's what they say. Then they start asking me questions. 'What really happened? — Did the man wear a mask?' "

"Soon die down," responded Verrell. "All this means more visitors, does it?"

"It does, sir. Though, of course, the place has been closed until yesterday afternoon/*

"Haven't had any bright ideas of your own since the last time I saw you?"

"Not likely, sir."

Diana spoke suddenly. "Richard, I've just remembered the address of that art dealer you wanted. At least, I know where I can find it."

"Jolly bonzer."

"What a ghastly expression."

"Supposed to be the rage. Or was it five years ago?"

"Stop talking drivel and come along and let's see if we can find it." She led the way.

Beach met them.

"Miss Diana, there's a 'phone call for you."

She excused herself, left, was gone more than ten minutes.

"Isn't that the sticky limit? Of all days, my best friend rings up and asks me to see her in London right away. Meeting her husband who's flying in from America first thing tomorrow. I haven't seen her in a month of Sundays, and "

"I hope you said yes."

"Well, I... as a matter of fact I did, Richard. I'm terribly sorry, but I won't be able to see her again in years. She lives up in Scotland."

"I can drop you in London."

"You really are the nicest person I know I"

"And since you'll be in London tomorrow, maybe we can go out together then."

"My friend isn't such a nuisance after all."

"Just before we dash off, Diana, could you get hold of that address?"

"Of course. Father has an old catalogue of theirs tucked away somewhere. I'll have a look while I'm changing."

The journey back to London was as quick as had been the drive down. When conditions were safe it did not scare Verrell to see the speedometer-needle hovering round the hundred mark. When they were unsafe he was, however, content to take things easily. Which was why he stayed alive.

"What time tomorrow can I expect you? Don't bother to move." Diana stepped out of the car and paused on the pavement.

" Sometime around elevenish suit you?"

"I'll be ready. Again many thanks." She waved, turned, and entered the building.

He drove away in the direction of South Kensington. To visit the art dealer whose address Diana had given him.

The shop had a small window space which contained only two canvases. Inside, it blossomed out into an emporium.

A man, in City garb of black coat and striped trousers, crossed the floor.

"Good afternoon, sir, may I help you?"

"I'm not quite sure," retorted Verrell easily, unperturbed by the other's professionally superior manner. "I've come to make enquiries about a painting I wish to purchase."

"Quite so, sir. We deal in paintings."

Verrell had a sense of humour described as puckish, or deplorable, according to the point of view of the person concerned.

"Do you really?" he enquired gravely.

The salesman blinked. "Yes, sir," he managed. Then he regained his composure. "What have you in mind, sir?" "You'd probably call it seventeenth-century type period. A fake."

"A... fake? Really, sir, that would hardly come within our province. Perhaps you would care to try somewhere else." "Your information is not quite accurate. You sold one not so very long ago." There was a snap in his voice.

"Sir, we do not sell fakes. This is an established firm; with a reputation." The man was becoming hot and bothered. "Bassete?"

The balloon was punctured. The righteous indignation vanished. "The Bassete... quite... quite different, sir." "My apologies. In my ignorance I thought he copied Van Dyck."

"That is true, sir. But when you mentioned fakes I hardly thought of his work. You see, sir, his copies were so brilliant that to some extent they rest on their own merits."

Verrell let the subtle difference slide. "Now that's cleared up, have you one for sale?"

"I regret, sir, no. We have only handled one, and to some extent," here the man coughed, "it was.a mistake. When we first contracted to buy it, we were of the impression that it 70

was genuine. It was not until we had examined it closely, and also taken expert advice, that we discovered the painting was a Bassete. By this time the owner was... well, in some straits, and pressed us to complete the purchase."

Verrell broke in. "What happened to the one you sold?"

"What happened, sir? I really don't know. A client bought it. I remember perfectly well, because one of the staff was "

"Would you be good enough to let me know this person's name and address. If I get in touch with him, he may be willing to sell."

The salesman assumed his remote expression for the second time. "I'm sorry, sir, we do not publish the result of negotiations into which we enter. Even if we had the name, we could not disclose it. Only yesterday I had a call from a most valued customer. He made the same request and I made the same answer. I... it was the same picture," he ended abruptly, and in amazement.

"You'd better try and get hold of some of the other Bassetes. He's rapidly coming into favour." Verrell laughed lightly. He should have known the other would not appreciate such a remark.

"We do not deal in..." Obviously he could not finish that sentence.

"You couldn't make an exception to this inflexible rule of yours? It's rather important I trace the painting."

"On no account, sir."

"That's that. Sorry to have troubled you."

"No trouble at all, sir. Anytime we can help you, please consult us."

"I'll let you know when I want to buy the Mona Lisa," he replied carelessly

"Sir, that painting is in the Louvre. I doubt very much whether..." But the customer had left.

The salesman returned to speak to his assistant.

"Really, a most peculiar man! First of all he wanted to buy a Bassete — then the Mona Lisa!"

Verrell returned to his car, sat down behind the wheel, lit a cigarette. The result of his visit was annoying, but not insurmountable. It was not the first time he had been balked in obtaining information by the ethical code of a dealer. On the last occasion it had meant his entombing himself inside a safe for a number of hours. This time things need not be quite so drastic.

At one stage of his visit to the art dealer a door had been opened at the back of the shop. Beyond it was an office. And he had just been able to catch sight of a large filing-cabinet. The answer might well be in that cabinet.

While he smoked he studied the street. It was a long one, containing many shops and stores. The entrance to the art dealer's was small; the door was set well back. The embrasure would provide cover — of sorts.

He drove off and circled the immediate block of shops. It was not a fruitful journey. As far as he could see the buildings stood back to back. It was the front of the shop... or nothing.

Midnight, and the streets were empty. Blackshirt drove his saloon car past the dealers', turned down a side street, parked it. He checked that his white scarf was securely in place, left the car and strode briskly along the pavement, turned into the main road.

Outside the small, unlit windows he paused. The road was still empty. Wasting no movement he stepped into the shallow entrance. He removed his scarf, pulled the hood on, eased the gloves over his fingers. Then rapidly, but so easily as to make his actions appear unhurried, he took a rubber pad and a glass-cutter from his pocket, pressed the pad against the centre of the glass door, drew a large circle round it with the cutter. A quick series of dull taps, and the circle came away, secured by the pad... It would have been quicker merely to unlock the door, but he had been unable to check for alarms that afternoon.

Blackshirt stepped inside, bringing the pane of glass after him, which he set back in position. Holding the rubber pad with one hand, he used the other to ease a strip of Selotape round the break. It held the glass in position.

He moved through the shop until he reached the door which gave access to the office, then switched the torch on. A quick check failed to reveal any alarms, and very slowly he 72

gripped the door-knob and turned it. As it came back to its fullest extent he pushed gently. There was a short explosive creak from the hinges — soon remedied by a generous application of oil. This time the door opened silently.

He entered the office, closed the door behind him. The beam of the torch showed a bare and impersonal room. Furniture had been reduced to a minimum. Two desks were placed at opposite ends, each had a typewriter and several bundles of papers. In between was the filing-cabinet.

He pulled out the drawer marked B and checked for the name Bassete, but drew a blank. He tried the Vs, found what he wanted. It was appropriate that the description of the painting was a work of art; Bassete, after the style of Van Dyck. He grinned. Perhaps it was as good a way of explaining things as any. The picture had been sold for the sum of sixty-five pounds to Mr. Jackson, Redroof, Gables Creek, near Dorking. Blackshirt made a note of the address, replaced the card, shut the cabinet drawer.

Five minutes later he stepped out of the front door, stripped off the hood and gloves, tied the white scarf round his neck, prepared to move away.

The sound of dragging feet checked him, and he leaned against the side of the entrance until a couple, too deep in their murmured conversation to notice anything short of an earthquake, passed by. When the road became deserted again, he stepped out and returned to his car. In a very short space of time he had garaged it and was walking blithely back to his flat. His concentration was nearly his undoing.

Jim and Parson had been sitting in the car for a long time. Their tempers were suffering.

"Make sure you don't miss the swine when he comes," snarled Jim. "I owes him something."

"Change the tune, can't you? We've heard nothing else for days except what you'll do to him when you get hold of him."

"Well?"

"Well nothing. You've had your chance. And missed it. If you'd done as I told you, we wouldn't be here now."

"I didn't miss nothing. It was Sam's fault!"

"That isn't his story. He said you let Verrell sling you round the room and couldn't do a thing about it."

"Swine never seems to go to bed." Jim changed the trend of the conversation. "Chasing round with the skirts somewhere. He'd better enjoy it — be the last time." He reached into his pocket and pulled out a large flask.

Parson half-turned. "Glad you've decided to be of some use! Shove it over; I could do with something to warm me up."

"Aren't we friendly all of a sudden?"

Parson had pulled a revolver out of his pocket. Then he mastered the sudden spurt of anger before it could do harm, and relaxed. "Keep it."

Jim took a noisy swallow of the neat whisky. "Keep your shirt on. Here, have a drop. I ain't a bloke to be mean."

After the drink came the inevitable cigarettes, handed out from a battered packet. The strain was telling on the two men. It showed by the haste with which they drew on the cigarettes.

"Can you shoot with that thing?" asked Jim.

"What the hell do you think? Attend to the car and leave the rest to me."

"Ain't no need to snap."

The two relapsed into sullen silence.

Jim broke it. "Here... That's him. Know his cock-a-hoop walk anywhere."

"Start the car. The moment I've fired get the hell away from here." Parson cocked the gun.

The walking figure came nearer.

Tension made them sweat.

"Why the hell's he walking so slowly?"

The distance closed to six yards. Parson could wait no longer. He stabbed his finger, and the bullet ploughed the pavement a foot to the right of the advancing figure.

Blackshirt moved with bewildering speed. He jumped to the right and ran at full pitch across the road, zig-zagging. Parson fired again and missed easily.

"Get out of here."

Jim needed no second bidding. The car at that moment turning into the road could easily be the police. He charged through the gears, heedless of bitter crunching, took the comer with tyres wailing.

Blackshirt halted. How narrow the escape had been he did not know. He'd remain content if he never met a narrower. Thoughtfully he entered his flat. The bidding for the stakes was beginning to grow.

Chapter Eight

By hurrying through his breakfast Verrell managed to arrive at Diana's fiat at the appointed time. It was soon evident that he might as well have arrived late. In common with others of her sex, she was not ready.

"Sit down, Richard. Choose a cigarette while I get ready."

"Thanks. Have a good evening?"

"No better and no worse than two old school friends ever have. We talked and talked. Freda's changed so much since she married that, really, one full evening of her is as much as I can take."

"Did you go out? Or wasn't there time between sentences?"

"No need to be sarcastic." She smiled. "We had dinner at a new place. Frightfully the thing to do. But it was quite awful." She began to describe the evening in some detail, stopped suddenly as she realized time was not standing still even if she was.

"I'm all set," she announced on her return.

He looked at his watch with an exaggerated gesture. "Not so bad. One and a half hours to put on a new face."

"You're quite disgusting, Richard. I'm not certain it's a good thing for me to be going out with you. A woman does not put on a new face. She gently emphasizes her good points. I have, not been an hour and a half. I've been jolly quick." She held her hand out. "Stop grousing and come on. Where are we going?"

"I thought we might drive down in the direction of Dorking. Unless, of course, you'd like to go somewhere else?"

"Yes, please, I want to go to Dover."

There was a pause. Diana laughed delightedly. "I was only joking, Richard. You want to go to Dorking, so we'll go. I wish you could have seen your face just then! What are we after, a new plot?"

"The answer to an old one," he answered, as they left the flat.

For lunch they chose an ancient inn tucked away in a forgotten village. The meal was simple, and suffered nothing by being so. They both showed some reluctance to move on.

"Where's this house we're going to, Richard?"

"Somewhere near here as far as I can make out. If we don't come across it soon we'd better stop and ask."

"Friend of yours live there?"

He spun the wheel over and took hard avoiding action against a local bus using nine-tenths of the road.

"No. But the owner has, or had, a painting by Bassete. I want to buy it from him."

"At this point my fatal feminine curiosity gets the better of me, and I have to ask why. But for heaven's sake don't answer if you'd rather not."

"That's kind of you," he answered lightly.

"Beast! You know something, Richard, you're up to no good. I was thinking about it yesterday. You know what?"

"No."

"You are the head of a large smuggling gang, sailing 'contraband across the Channel twice a week. You bring in spirits and wine, nylon stockings, and Dior dresses. The last items you hand round to all your friends. If you don't hurry up with the latest creation in gold *lame* I'll send an anonymous letter to the Commissioner of Police."

He laughed. "You're wrong. About the dresses. I favour Balenciaga. *And* I only give them to people I like!"

"Very well. If that's the way you feel."

Verrell braked suddenly. "Signpost said to the right. Give a yell if anything comes up."

They backed, turned, continued slowly. Five hundred yards along the road they came to a small village where he stopped and asked a farm labourer, in charge of a horse and cart, the way to the house.

"Straight on 'til you comes to the pond, then left, and it's the first house past the hay-field."

To their surprise the directions were correct.

The name, Redroof, was not a misnomer, merely a written description of the complete vulgarity. The roof was not brick-red, but a flaming crimson which would cause comment in California. The green paint, the long French windows set beneath a transom window of stained glass, the lack of proportion in the squat building, merely assisted the roof to complete a monstrosity.

"Golly!" murmured Diana. "All change at Clapham 76

Common. Owner must be colour-blind, or mentally defective. I wonder if it just grew, or whether someone really had the nerve to build it. Look at this gate, Richard; wrought-iron cupids."

"This was worth coming for! Let us get out and see what kind of human lives inside."

They left the car. He opened the gates and waited for her to pass through. "It ought to be listed as one of the historic buildings."

The drive was circular. They crossed it, reached the front door almost hidden under a porch of Homeric dimensions. Verrell rang the bell. Faintly, they heard the muffled tones of a musical chime. There was silence. He tried again.

"Have we come all this way, endured what we have seen, only to find the owner out?"

"Not very promising, is it? Still, we can have a try at the back just in case they're round that way and can't hear us."

They walked round a garden beginning to show signs of neglect. The tradesmen's entrance was unadorned. Verrell gave a couple of quick knocks with the solid brass knocker, was amazed when the door opened.

A small woman looked at them. She was small from tip to toe, had a face that just missed being miniature perfection.

"Yes?" Her voice betrayed her as a foreigner.

"Is Mr. Jackson in?"

"No." She spoke flatly, without expression. It spoilt the attractive picture she made.

"Do you know when he will be back?"

"He won't."

Verrell stifled a sigh. He thought it probable she did not understand what he said. "Are you Mrs. Jackson?"

"I am not. I am the maid."

He had been watching her closely as she spoke. For the first time an expression crossed her eyes. A strange, almost vicious look.

"I've come down from London especially to see him. Would you tell me how I might get in touch with him?" He smiled.

"I do not know."

"Chatty," said Diana in an undertone. "Tell you her life story in the first five minutes."

"Will he be back here?"

"I have said he will not."

Verrell eased his hand through his hair. It was like talking to the Sphinx. Unfortunately, she gave the impression that she could continue very much longer than he could.

He tried again. "Does Mr. Jackson own this house?"

"He did."

"Who owns it now?"

"I do not know."

"For heaven's sake, Richard, there must be several screws loose. Try words of one syllable." Diana, growing more and more impatient, stopped trying to hide the fact.

The woman looked at her bleakly.

Verrell quickly resumed his questioning. "Has Mr. Jackson sold the house?"

"No."

"Then he must own it," he remarked reasonably.

"Must he?"

"Of course."

"I do not know." She had retired to the safety of her favourite phrase. It was like a record. Then, suddenly, it changed. "Why do you want to know?"

"Because, as I've been trying to point out, I want to see him."

"Why?"

"What the deuce is that to do with her?" asked Diana. He decided to be more diplomatic, much as he would have liked to have followed his companion's lead. "I believe Mr. Jackson collected paintings?"

"No!" Her voice rose sharply. Her face moved... Then everything was under control again. "He does not."

'Here we go round the mulberry-bush,' he thought in desperation. 'Any sentence which explains anything is forbidden.' "But he has some paintings?"

"Maybe."

"I'm asking this for a special reason." He smiled at her. "I have a friend who collects paintings, and quite by chance I told him I was trying to get hold of a particular one. He said that Mr. Jackson had bought one some time ago. It may be rather an impertinence, but I've come along to ask your employer if he would be willing to sell it to me."

Suddenly the woman smiled. It made her all the more incredible, since it was one of the most unconvincing expressions he had ever seen.

"YrTi^are an art-collector?" she asked.

"Only in a very small way."

"What is your name?"

"I was coming to that. If I give you a card, perhaps you would be kind enough to give it to Mr. Jackson. If you would explain what it is all about, and ask him to get in touch with me."

"He will not be back. But you have a card?"

Verrell took out his wallet and handed one to her. She took it, dropped it into a pocket without bothering to read it.

"Would you mind doing that for me?"

"I shall do as you ask." Her voice was almost mocking. "The painting you want. What is it, who is it by?"

"Bassete, though at the time it was thought to be Van Dyck. If you would just say that I would like to buy it and am willing to offer a very generous amount."

"How generous?"

"I will discuss that with Mr. Jackson," he said, with a trace of asperity.

"Perhaps!"

Without another word or look she shut the door.

"If that isn't the finest exhibition of a trained lunatic I've ever seen," snapped Diana. "When you see this chap just you tell him what you think. If one of our servants dared to answer a visitor like that we'd have something to say."

"She's a foreigner. Probably doesn't quite know what's what. Maybe she's only just come here."

"Then if she were in my employ I'd make certain she left quickly."

"You're very bitter."

She turned, and regarded him with a strained expression on her face. "If ever I've hated anyone, it's that woman. Why, I haven't an earthly. It's just that... Richard, I'm being very silly."

He grinned sympathetically. "Can't say I fell in love with her at sight. She'd be more in place in a haunted castle. Still, if the elusive Jackson likes her around to deepen the gloom, it's his funeral. Let's get moving to other climes."

They returned to the car and drove off. Verrell retraced his steps. He expected to reach the main road after passing through the village. In fact, after a quarter of an hour's driving, a possibility became a probability. He harf Tost his way.

"Well, I'm damned!" he muttered indignantly. "I always thought I had a sense of direction."

"From the look of these lanes even the locals need a guide. I could have sworn we'd been here before!"

They had. As he immediately realized.

"Our journey reaches classical proportions. This happens to be the opposite end of the road from which we started. Diana, we are in grave danger. I forgot to pack food and drink. If we are not found soon..." he tailed off.

A car, small and old, turned out of the drive of Redroof and went up the road away from them. A woman had been driving. A small woman, since even in that car she had been almost lost behind the steering-wheel.

The idea which had been hovering round his mind settled. It wouldn't be necessary to take the painting away now he knew where to look.

He stopped the car. "Do you mind if I leave you for a sec.? I knew there was something I'd forgotten to mention, and there may still be someone inside."

"Go right ahead. If you get a reception like last time, call for me and I'll tell her what I think."

He left her, walked up to the front door. His ringing produced no effect. He tried the back door, but as that too was unanswered he felt fairly certain the place was empty. He checked on his driving-gloves to make certain no tear could leave any portion of flesh exposed, made a mental note to destroy them as soon as he reached home. He took a penknife out of his pocket.

The windows were latched. He undid the smaller of the knife-blades, edged it between the two window frames, pushed the catch back.

In under the minute he was inside the house. With some surprise he realized the furnishings showed taste. Against the wall of the dining-room was a tapestry which could be a genuine Gobelins of the eighteenth century. There was a companion one in the drawing-room. A small study was lined 80

with books bound in fine leather which made a rich, warm furnishing. In the hall was a Tompion clock. The farther he went the more it became obvious that the owner was a man of wealth.

Upstairs, the main bedroom had a fine Savonnerie carpet. Its glowing colours blended perfectly with the hand embroidered silk bedspread.

The other bedrooms were well, if not equally well, furnished. But the house lacked one thing. Life. There was no suggestion that anyone lived there. Nothing was out of place. Not a single magazine or newspaper was lying around. It was like a show-place waiting for the public.

It also lacked something more important. That was the Bassete painting. He found two Renoirs, unless someone else had taken up forgery on a large scale, a Turner, and three of a variety which had to be seen to be believed. Which was all very interesting, but useless.

He returned downstairs, had a last check round, then re-locked the window by which he had entered. The back door had a self-locking catch, and slipped shut as he closed the door behind him.

He reached the gates; started. Talking to Diana was a police-constable.

"Were they in?" she asked.

"You tell me. I kept ringing and no one answered, but that may mean anything considering the way the old girl acted before."

"I've just been asking the constable the way to the main road. We went wrong at the fork; should have borne right instead of left."

Verrell thanked the policeman. "We were beginning to wonder if we should ever see home again."

"There're some funny mix-ups in the roads round here," he agreed. "And the sign-posting ain't all that helpful. I see you've been up to Redroof, sir."

Veirell's face gave no hint of the questions the last statement had produced in his mind. It seemed casual enough — but it was often the most casual question which held the most snares.

"Yes," he answered simply.

Diana was more exact. "We did. And what's more we ran into a most peculiar woman. Every time we asked her where Mr. Jackson was she said she didn't know. Began to think he must be a poltergeist."

The constable carefully used a handkerchief to mop his brow. "You aren't the only one, miss," he said, as he replaced the handkerchief.

"How do you mean?"

"I mean, miss, that what we'd like to know in the Force is whether this man is alive or dead. Or as you said, one of them things which haunts houses."

"Is he missing?" broke in Verrell.

"He is and he ain't," answered the other. "Leastways, be more correct to say we don't know."

Diana laughed. "This gets more and more complicated! What's it all about — or is that a secret?"

"It's a long story, miss. Though if you don't mind listening to it, then I don't mind telling it."

"You carry on. Just about up your street, Richard; do as a plot for one of your books. Title: Was He Dead? A large question mark."

"Do you write, sir?"

"Yes. Name's Richard Verrell."

He had met so many people who pretended to know his name, it was a delight to meet one who really did.

"*The* Richard Verrell, sir?"

He laughed. "The only one I know of, anyway!"

"Well, sir, this is a surprise." The constable was obviously delighted, and a trifle awed. "Many's the book of yours I've had out of the library and enjoyed every word of it. Being a policeman, one thing I likes is a book that's accurate. Now, sir, take that last book of yours where the man breaks into the house. Wasn't a word that couldn't be true."

The constable was more accurate than he knew. The book had described one of Blackshirt's exploits quite well.

"This is a pleasure, sir. I hope you don't mind my saying so?"

"Rather not. Music to the ears."

"And if what I tell you is any use, then I hope you'll send me a copy of the book, sir."

"Check! But look, if it's a long story won't we be keeping?"

"'Bless me, no, sir. I'm off duty, so me time's me own."

Verrell looked at his watch. "Pity, still twenty minutes to opening time. Unless you open early round these parts?"

The constable grinned. It was a smile which spread and spread. "We do and we don't, sir. You come along with me." Here he winked with fervour.

"Good," said Diana, "I'm parched. And it's sure to taste better if we're breaking the law."

The constable merely winked the harder. "Up this road is the King's Arms. You carry on, sir, and I'll be along presently. And if you have something lined up like, then I won't be the one to complain!"

They did as had been suggested. The landlord poured out two pints of beer, and a half-pint of cider. Almost as soon as he had done so the policeman arrived.

"Hullo, Joe, feeling thirsty?"

From the way they both laughed, it was obviously a parish joke.

"Here's how," said Verrell, passing over one of the pint glasses.

"Your health, sir. Nothing like a pint of beer on a hot day." He drank deeply. "I was going to tell you about Jackson. If you can make head or tail of the affair, then, sir, I'd like to hear about it. For none of us can. Isn't that right, Bert?"

"That's so," agreed the bartender.

"This chap, he comes along and buys the house just after the war. Paid a mint of money for it. Village talk has it that he was an Austrian who spent a number of years in a concentration camp. As I say, he bought this house and lived there with his wife, and that maid you disliked, miss."

"And how," she murmured.

"None of the villagers liked them. They did keep very much to themselves, didn't they, Bert?"

"That they did," the other agreed. "Never seen them in here."

"Three weeks ago, come tomorrow, Mr. Jackson had a car accident. He had two cars, and one of them was as big as a house. Bentley, I think it was. My mate was going round the lanes one night when he came across this big car in the ditch, leastwise, what was left of it. Burnt to a cinder it was. And so was the man inside."

The constable paused, lifted up his glass, and with a mighty swallow finished the contents. There was no hesitation in accepting a refill.

"'Of course, we had to get the wife along to identify the body. She took it a lot more calmly than what I thought, but then she was a foreigner also," he said with satisfaction. "There was one bit of flesh what wasn't burnt, and it had a scar on it. She took one look at this scar and said yes, it was her husband."

"But I thought you said you didn't know whether he was alive or not," cut in Diana.

"No more we do, miss. I was coming to that."

"Don't interrupt," grinned Verrell. "Especially as the plot is thickening."

"And that ain't putting it too mildly, sir. His wife swore it was him. And if you asks me, the way she took the news, she wasn't any too sorry. Things was like that for three days." He paused for effect. "Then into the bank where he keeps his account walks Mr. Jackson."

Diana drew in her breath sharply.

"Thought that would interest you, miss. He walked in; says he wanted to take out a painting he'd kept there for safety."

It was Verrell's turn to start. "What kind of painting?"

"That I don't rightly know. Must have been valuable, though, to put it in a bank. Of course the place gave it to him. They hadn't heard of the accident, being in a large town like. He said thank you, and walks out with it. And that's the last anyone has heard of him!"

"Nobody's seen him since?" she asked.

"Not a single person, miss. Of course the police tried to check where he went to. They spoke to the railway staff, taxi-drivers, bus drivers… but it weren't no good. He just vanished."

"Interesting," remarked Verrell, a far-away look in his eyes.

"Quite, sir, though it ain't the word I'd use myself. Why didn't he come back, if he was alive? If he were, why did his wife recognize the scar? Nothing wrong in the house that we could find. Bank says his account with them totals more than I'll ever see. But that still ain't the end of all this."

"Don't say he got killed again," suggested Diana.

"No, miss. Not he. But his wife did!"

"She's dead?"

"More than that. Murdered. I found her between here and her house, and it fair turned me up. She'd been hit on the head with a large piece of wood. I called the sergeant, he called the inspector, and before you knew what's what everybody was tripping over everybody else's feet, taking photos and measurements, and Lord knows what else."

"Did you find the murderer?" asked Diana.

"No, miss. Not a thing. We haven't discovered a thing from that day to this."

"What's happening to the maid who's so chatty?"

"She keeps around, miss, but beyond that I don't know. Don't believe she's got a drop of blood in her. All ice-water. When we told her what had happened, all she did was to say 'yes', calm as you like."

The glasses were empty.

"Would you care for another one?" asked Verrell.

"Thank you, no, sir. Have one more and the wife would accuse me of being under the influence when I get back." His voice sank. "She has no sense of humour," he explained.

"Thanks, anyway, for the story."

"What can you make of it, sir?"

"Not much," admitted Verrell. "Right now the job of sorting it all out is a bit too complicated."

"I'm going to say thank you, sir, for the drop of beer, and get back to the wife. And if ever you use this, then you won't forget your promise, will you, sir?"

"Write your name and address on this piece of paper."

The constable grinned his thanks as Verrell and Diana left in the car.

"A penny for them?" she smiled.

"They're worth more than that. There aren't all that number of Bassete paintings around!"

Chapter Nine

They made excellent time back to London despite a convoy of army lorries which drove on the principle that they were bigger than anything else on the road, so what the hell?

"A meal is indicated," said Verrell. "I feel like going Indian — say anything to you?"

"It does."

"Good." He looked at his watch. "We might as well make tracks. By the time we've downed a sherry the hour will be just right."

Diana looked pained. "I've got to go back to the flat and change. I couldn't possibly go out looking like this!"

To his masculine eyes she looked perfect enough. However, without showing too much amazement, he drove her back and patiently waited while she prepared herself for dinner.

Later that night, he dropped her back at her flat after a most pleasant meal.

"It's all been very sweet of you, Richard. I've enjoyed every minute of the day; especially when the constable came to the grisly bits and looked suitably macabre. You still haven't said whether you've got any ideas on the subject." "One or two," he admitted.

"Such as? Stop imitating a clam."

"Very well. One, Mr. Jackson is either dead or alive."

She laughed. "That's one statement nobody could argue with."

"If you would let me finish…" he protested with mock annoyance.

"Very well."

"Either he died in the car, or the corpse was someone else's dressed in his clothes."

"And with his identifying scar?"

"Stop making things difficult. Besides, if he appears at the bank later, it could hardly have been he in the car."

"Maybe it was someone imitating him."

"I doubt whether it would be possible to do that in broad daylight at a place where they'd be doubly careful. Then again, he'd have to sign a receipt for the picture and there're mighty few people who can forge a signature while under observation."

"All right — so he was at the bank. Why did his wife identify him in the car?"

"Maybe she didn't like him. Or else wanted to investigate his possessions."

"Don't be silly, Richard. If it wasn't the husband, it wouldn't be any good identifying him for that very reason. Next thing would be he'd turn up and want to know what was what. Besides, she got killed herself."

"She wouldn't have known that at the time, would she?"

"I don't know. The whole thing seems upside down to me, and I'm much too tired to worry about it now. You've disappointed me, Richard; I was looking to you for the answer."

"Sorry and all that. Ask me the next time I see you."

"That's a date. By the way, I've had an invitation to a dance next month. Would you care to partner me? Can't promise what it will be like, but the Craigs generally put up a good show."

"Thanks, sounds fine."

"Good. I'll give you the details later."

He left and returned to his flat. Lit a cigarette and lay back in a chair. The story of Jackson was intriguing. So many whys.

Why appear to be burnt in a car? To vanish without trace? Then why appear at the bank? Why take only a painting from the bank? If he was going to vanish he must have needed money. Did he know it was a Bassete? If so, he must have known what it was worth. That was, other than as a painting.

His last assumption seemed almost cast-iron. The other paintings in the house were far more valuable than the one he had stored at the bank. If he knew it was only a Bassete, why should he store it in safety and leave the others? Surely, because he was aware of the special circumstances. Might he think it really was a Van Dyck? Hardly. The art dealer had sold it to him for sixty-five pounds. He could hardly imagine he had secured a genuine Van Dyck for that price. No! Almost certainly Jackson knew the painting was a Bassete, knew its connection with the von Steiner affair.

The implication hit him in no uncertain measure. He cursed himself for not having seen it before. He might be jumping before the gate; there might be no gate. But…

He stubbed the cigarette out and left the flat at speed. His Healey had hardly begun to cool, sprang into life at the first touch of the starter. With a wheel-spin which punished the tyres, he left and, heedless of speed-limits, raced along the roads.

Diana's flat was on the ground floor, and was large and luxurious, though she referred to it as her tiny place in London. He pressed the bell and waited, hoping he had been stumbling round in a mare's-nest. There was no response. He tried again, mentally working out how long it would take her to wake up and reach the door.

The lock stayed shut for as long as it took him to get a skeleton-key out of his pocket. He stepped inside the flat and closed the door. Rapidly he moved through until he came to the bedroom. The bed had not been touched, the cover was still on it.

The flat was empty. Despite a careful search he could find nothing to indicate whether she had left it voluntarily or involuntarily. There was nothing more he could do, and he left. Hoping for the best.

Back at his flat he 'phoned her, waited a full five minutes before replacing the receiver. He checked on the time, realized it was almost midnight.

The score was not so good. He thought about getting in touch with Sir Edward. At that point his own telephone rang.

"Yes?"

"Is that Mr. Verrell speaking?" The caller was a woman. The wires distorted the voice, but he still caught a peculiar flatness, a lack of expression. It did not need a team and twenty questions to guess her identity. The maid they had met at Redroof that afternoon had been all too singular.

"It is."

"Do you know who I am, Mr. Verrell?"

"I do not."

"Or why?"

"What do you want? I'm just about to go to bed."

"Mr. Verrell, in the short time I met you I judged you to be moderately intelligent. In that case don't be in too much 88

of a hurry to go to bed. I have a business proposition to make. I think it will interest you/'

"Who's speaking?"

"Very well — if you insist. You met me this afternoon. I was the maid who had to answer your questions. You wouldn't know my name because I did not give it to you. I know yours because you very kindly gave it to me.

I also know your companion's since she has been photographed sufficiently frequently to be easily recognized."

"I still don't "

"You are a fool, Mr. Verrell. Or should I say that you are trying to act like one?"

"Why?" He reached for a cigarette; thereby ignoring gloomy prophecies of tortured lungs. He needed a pick-me-up. To throw an ace away to a lowly trump was infuriating as well as stupid.

"Because you try to treat me as one. And because you walked blithely up to the house and asked me if Mr. Jackson had a painting by Bassete. I expect you would like to buy it, but our price would be much too high. What made you think we would be taken in by so silly a request?"

"It was genuine."

"Of course. I'm only doubting the sense of your motives. But to get down to more serious matters. I want the painting you have."

He drew in a deep breath of smoke, let it trickle out through his nostrils before answering. "Which painting?"

"Mr. Verrell, I have been very patient. For everybody's sake don't try to see just how patient I can be. You stole one from the Freshman collection. Very clever of you; it proves you are not a complete idiot. I want it."

She was wrong, misinformed, and hopelessly out of date. Though how that was going to help was anybody's guess. His canvas came from the Old Masters' Gallery. Who had the Freshman one was something he'd give a lot to know.

"Are you still there?"

"I am."

"Listen carefully. You will give me that painting. Naturally, I don't expect to get it for nothing. When you were stupid enough to come to the house you said you wanted to buy the Bassete we had. You will not mind if we now discuss the price of the one you're selling. At the moment Miss Freshman, while not liking her new quarters — she's staying with me for the present — is still unharmed. If I get the painting you have, she will stay that way. A good bargain. One Bassete against one young and attractive lady."

"I admire the use of the word bargain," he replied. "Excellent. I was prepared to deal with a flood of angry threats. Conventional and useless. We begin to understand each other, I see."

"Don't put it that high," he snapped.

"As the French would say, *du calme*. Your friend has made several offensive remarks during the short time she's been with me, but so far I have ignored them. Don't try my patience too far."

"Very well."

"Good. To come back to this painting."

"Certainly. But I still haven't got it."

"Stop playing the idiot." Her voice rose out of its normal flatness.

"I know nothing about it. Neither who took it, nor where it is now."

"A pity. You make me feel sorry for you. And even more sorry for Miss Freshman." She paused, then continued. "You do not know my real name?"

"No."

"In Germany I was known as Schmidt. A common name, but there, we can't choose. Paula Schmidt."

It might be a common name, but it was yet not easily forgotten. The concentration camps of the war were hell-spots, with little to choose between them for brutality, degradation, and slaughter. But one stood out; a vicious landmark notorious even among the others. It was a camp for women, staffed by women, commanded by a woman. Paula Schmidt.

Her rule had made the record of the Spanish Inquisition appear the work of bungling amateurs. At the end of the war it had been reasonable to suppose she would reap what she had sewn. But from the day she walked out of the camp, two hours ahead of the invading Allied forces, nothing more had been heard of her.

"The deep silence means recognition?"

"It does."

Back came a short laugh. "Then all we have to do is to arrange matters. You will have the painting ready, and do exactly as I tell you. I want it precisely as you found it. If you've been rash enough to take anything out of the frame, replace it."

"For the last time I have not got the painting which came from the Freshman collection."

She ignored him completely. "Tomorrow you will wait until I 'phone you. I will then tell you where to meet me. Bring the painting along. I will take it back with me and check it. If everything is in order, then your dear friend can return to you. Have I made myself clear?"

"Yes." He stabbed the cigarette out, hardly aware of the fact that the last half of it had smouldered away.

"Then good night. It has been a pleasure talking to you." The line went dead.

He replaced the receiver slowly. One stupid slip had landed him in a quagmire. Admittedly there had been nothing to indicate that, when he visited the Jackson home, he was putting his head into a hornet's nest. But he had ignored the fact that there might be more than two people after the same thing. His brain should have worked more quickly when the constable told his story.

Then, characteristically, he stopped the post-mortem dead in its tracks. The question mark pointed to the future. The woman wanted a Bassete painting — the one from the Freshman collection. He could have offered her his own copy, and the odds were she would not have known the difference, but he had told Roberts to clear away what was left of the frame after he had taken it to pieces.

He could offer the vital slip of paper, and hope the woman would keep her bargain. But that would be surrendering the fort without firing a gun. He paced the floor, trying to reach a solution.

The woman wanted a painting and was going to arrange a meeting. The call he had just received had been a local one, judging by the way it had come straight through without any operator's assistance. She was in London. Not very hopeful. And yet it might be. If he could hand the painting over it should be possible to find out where she was taking it. Not a job for him. More than one person would be needed. It could be done, given some split-second timing...

There was still the painting. When he handed it over, she would make a cursory check. If he tried faking (he grinned wryly) the damage would be done before he could lift a finger. Time was too short. He stopped pacing, irritated to be stymied so easily.

Another five minutes, then suddenly he smiled. It was difficult to see how he could have taken so long to reach the obvious solution. Bassete had copied Van Dyck. It was time Van Dyck copied Bassete!

He knew of one genuine Van Dyck. The Gallery of Old Masters! The familiar sense of excitement caught him up.

The police would take note if the alarms went off throughout the night. There was no chance of working the same trick again. What other way was there of forcing an entry? He sat down, considered the plan of the building.

The idea came from nowhere. It was complete when it arrived. The police would be ready for anything the next time the alarm sounded. They would be keyed-up, expecting another attempt on the paintings, and would stick like bulldogs around the Gallery. Just the moment to convince them they had been tricked into staying put. That the real trouble was elsewhere.

How to be in two places at once? He thought a piece of string, a tin, and some powder of the more destructive type would provide a solution.

A quick check outside confirmed that there was no wind. He raided his medicine-cabinet and took out a packet of saltpetre, dissolved it in a basin of water, soaked a length of string in the mixture. Then, he lit the oven and put the string inside to dry.

In his drawer was a carton half-full of twelve-bore cartridges, legacy of a visit to the country. He took as many as were left, cut them open, spilled the black granules into a tin.

The string was soon dry, forming the fuse for the extempore bomb. He adjusted it to burn for three minutes, after a couple of short experiments.

Blackshirt changed rapidly, left the flat and made his way to one of the streets which led out of the square which enclosed 92

the Gallery. In it was a jeweller's shop. He worked quickly, thankful the iron gate was recessed sufficiently to allow him to work out of sight of the road. He placed the tin inside the gate, pushed the fuse into the small hole in the lid, ran the end back along the entry and lit it.

To the side of the back door of the Gallery, which Blackshirt had used so successfully, was a tree, planted when the building was new, and which had grown older far more gracefully. Its trunk would just about afford him sufficient protection. The police were not fools, and they had had plenty of time in which to discover how the previous theft had been carried out.

He checked his watch. One-and-a-half minutes to go, and time for the fun to begin. He unlocked the side door, opened it, slammed it shut, moved with speed into the shelter of the tree.

Procedure at first followed the orthodox pattern. The police came out of the station quicker, if anything, than they had done the very first time.

The same sergeant was in command. "Get round this building and stay round until we've searched it from top to bottom. The Where in the hell are those watchmen?"

As if in answer the two men appeared at the opened door.

"Anyone inside?" barked the sergeant.

"Not this time."

"Keep a damned good eye skinned then."

"All right, no need to tell us our job."

The sergeant ignored the rejoinder. He checked that the others were moving to their allotted positions. One constable was within five feet of the tree trunk, behind which Blackshirt sheltered, when the bomb went off.

In the quiet of the deserted streets it sounded as though the I.R.A. had disposed of the House of Commons and the Law Courts in one fell swoop. The explosion echoed and reechoed and thumped its way round the square. It was a stirring tribute to the maker.

"Good God! What...?" The sergeant was momentarily stunned by the sudden noise.

Blackshirt chose the moment. "The jeweller's," he shouted excitedly. "They're going for the jeweller's."

The sergeant shook hesitation to one side. Fiercely he tugged his whistle from his pocket and blew a sharp blast.

"Get to Macey," he yelled at the top of his voice. "Smash and grab."

The men turned and raced towards the jeweller's, cursing the fact that they had been tricked once more.

The two guards watched them go.

"This spot's becoming more like Piccadilly," observed one.

"YouTe right there. Been here twenty years next "

His interesting reminiscences were interrupted. Abruptly.

"Turn round, keep your hands away from your pockets," Blackshirt snapped. He dug a rigid forefinger into the back of the nearest man.

"Here "

"Turn, or I'll blast you." He was enjoying himself.

The guards liked their skins the way they had them. Without hesitation they turned.

"Get inside."

They got.

"Stop."

They were opposite the small room used for brewing their tea.

"Inside, and on the floor."

They lay down on their stomachs. For one it was an action as difficult as it was unusual.

"At the first sign of a movement I'll chop you." Rightly, or wrongly, Blackshirt thought he was using authentic talk. Satisfied that everything was under control he moved away, noiselessly.

He took the Van Dyck off the wall and wrapped it up in a sheet of paper. He returned to the small room and looked at the prostrate men.

"I'm watching you," he cautioned them, before he left.

It was some time before the sergeant returned to the Gallery. In his notebook was a full report of what had happened. He was congratulating himself on having stopped any suggestion of another burglary. Before going in to tell the guards what had happened, he paused. A strong believer in the old maxim 'give praise where praise is due', he called Fenton over.

"Good bit of work, me lad, coming to so quickly. Not that I wasn't about to say the same thing!"

"Come to over what?"

"Yelling out and making the men get a move on to the jeweller's. No knowing what might have been pinched."

Fenton looked surprised. "Wasn't me that shouted, Sergeant. Came from ahead of me."

"There wasn't anyone ahead of you," the other pointed out.

"Then who…?"

The sergeant moved with speed. He might just as well have taken his time. It was a sad sight.

Verrell admired the painting. If it were possible he'd send it back to its home once it had served its purpose. It was with some misgivings, then, that he checked the number of a private 'phone and prepared to make a call. Wright would, if at home, be fast asleep. He was not the type of man to wake up gladly in the middle of the night. But his assistance was necessary. And although Wright was connected with the special work of the police, Blackshirt had done him the best of deeds twice. It was really only a little quid pro quo.

The ringing note continued for some time before the connection was through.

"Yes?" Wright sounded as he felt.

Verrell grinned. "What's the time?" he asked.

"What the hell? Who's that?"

"No need to get annoyed."

"By God, I'll get this call traced back and stop your nonsense."

"You can't! Anyway, can't you take a joke?"

It became rapidly obvious Wright could not.

He took pity. "Verrell speaking."

There was an explosive snort. "I might have known it! Only one man in this country with such a warped sense of humour. Mark my words, Verrell, I'll run you in for this."

The other laughed. He was not too dismayed. The two men might have been close friends, despite their dissimilar characters, had they not worked on different sides of the fence. Even in these circumstances each had a strong regard for the other, and although Wright would see Blackshirt broken a dozen times if it were necessary to reach his goal — when that goal was attained, then he was perfectly sincere in his admiration.

"I'm not waking you up to wish you a merry Christmas. I want you to do me a favour if you will."

"No." There was no hesitation.

"You sound sour."

"The Lord preserve me! You wake me in the middle of the night and have the nerve to say Im sour. I hope youTe in gaol and wanting a reference. I'll see you damn well stay there."

"I'm not in gaol."

"Blast!"

"Have you a couple of men I could borrow tomorrow, probably in the morning?"

"Why?"

"I want a spot of help."

"What kind of trouble have you landed yourself in this time?"

"None. It's someone else's."

" 'Phone the police."

Verrell laughed. "Number's engaged. You'd be doing me a great favour," he added after a pause.

"That's quite enough to put me off completely. What do you want them to do? Pinch the Crown Jewels?"

"If they've got time, yes. First of all I want to know where a woman I'm meeting lives."

"Where are you meeting her?"

"I don't know yet. She's going to 'phone me. If I could let you know as soon as she tells me?"

"If I'm not in the office ask for McGrath and tell him. He'll know what to do."

"I must know where the woman lives the moment your men find out. And if it looks as though they're going some way away from the meeting-spot I want to be able to start moving in that direction."

Wright sighed heavily. "You don't want much! Arrange a check point for them to call back."

"Thanks."

"Is that all, now?" he asked sarcastically.

"For the moment."

"Then maybe you'll let me get some sleep."

The line clicked dead.

Chapter Ten

Paula Schmidt rang at nine o'clock the next morning. Verrell was having breakfast.

"Good morning, you slept well?"

"Perfectly, thank you," he replied. "I trust the same can be said for your guest?"

She chuckled. "To some extent I admire your choice. There has been no wailing and gnashing of teeth. Instead, the attractive Diana has spent a great part of the time telling me to go to hell in picturesque language. It's amazing how these well-brought-up young ladies learn such things."

"I'm glad she's up to it."

"So I imagine. For her sake I hope she doesn't try my temper too much. I remember one woman I had in my charge who came from a well-connected family. Her father was stupid enough to join a plot against the Fiihrer. That girl's spirit lasted three days."

He didn't bother to make any remark. The silence piqued her.

"I hope you enjoyed my little story?*'

"You may rest assured."

"I'm beginning to like you. There's a trace of German rationalism in you. I suppose you are English?"

"I am."

"Strange. Now, with regard to this painting. You have it ready for me?"

"Yes."

"Excellent. Wrap it up in brown paper. Whilst you're doing that make certain it won't take me too long to check. For everybody's sake I ought to return in good time. You understand that?"

"Perfectly."

"It is now just after nine. Your flat is near Hyde Park, which will be as good a meeting-place as any. Arrive at Marble Arch Underground Station at ten-thirty exactly, enter the park through the main gates, and turn sharp left. Somewhere along that stretch you'll meet me. Shall I repeat that?"

"You don't have to bother." He kept his voice level.

"One last word. Despite your ridiculous bluff last night when you said you had no painting, I'm convinced you're intelligent. I shall not, therefore, go to all the trouble of telling you what will happen should anything go wrong."

"I have a good imagination."

She laughed. "I doubt if it would be good enough on this occasion."

He paced the floor after she had rung off. More worried than he would have admitted. He proposed to pit Diana's life against the small slip of paper he had found in the Bassete painting. It was loading the dice too heavily. Too much could go wrong. Wright's men might make one slip and Diana... He'd got one of the pieces of paper — wasn't the only sensible course to hand it over and trust the other half of the bargain would be kept?

Logic answered the question. Since when had people like Paula Schmidt kept their bargains? Diana was something that, of necessity, had to be destroyed. Come to that, he was in the same category. If he handed the slip of paper over, Paula would thank him — possibly. She would depart. And that would be that. Diana would never leave the file of missing persons.

He walked across to his 'phone, dialled.

"Wright?"

"Here. That you, Verrell?"

"I've just had the message."

"Good. I arrived here eaily in case. You sounded pretty grim so I want to make certain nothing slips up."

"Damned decent of you."

"Rubbish! Do the same for anyone." A magnificent lie which deceived neither speaker nor listener. "What's happening?"

"Meeting in Hyde Park just after half past ten. I have to leave Marble Arch Station at the half-hour, enter the main gates, turn left. She'll pick me up somewhere along that road. Where we go after that — if anywhere — I don't know. I'll be carrying a parcel which I have to hand over to her."

"Give me a description of her."

He rapidly gave a comprehensive sketch.

"No idea where she'll be heading after the party?"

"None. Practically certain it will be somewhere in London.

She may have her car up here. A small black Austin Seven Ruby."

"Number?"

"I don't know."

"That seems to be all. I'll get things in hand right away. What about a check point? Suggest you come round to the office here. I'll have a car waiting. Something a little less disgusting than that red beast of yours, but every bit as fast."

"If it's no bother, it's a good idea."

"Of course it's a bother," snapped Wright. "The whole thing is completely upsetting my entire day. Had to call men in from all sorts of jobs."

"You won't need more than two, will you?"

"You attend to your business and I'll look after my end. Try covering a place like the park with two men! Chuck that sort of stuff down in your books, but if you don't want this good lady of yours to know what's happening it'll take every man jack I'm putting on."

"They know it's…"

"Yes. Whatever you were going to say. Now leave me some peace to get organized."

Verrell tried to thank him again, found he was talking to a dead line.

Time dragged. Just before he was about to leave, the telephone rang and Roberts answered it. Sir Edward Freshman was trying to trace his daughter. Verrell shook his head quickly. In smooth tones Roberts announced that his master was out, but that he would take any message there might be.

Ten-thirty. He stepped out of the tube-station, crossed the road, entered the park. Three hundred yards along Paula, small, precise, rose from a seat.

"This is a pleasure, Mr. Verrell. I'm glad to see you have carried out my instructions as precisely as one would expect you to. Now, come for a short walk with me. We'll cross here, and go over this grass which always seems so incongruous in a filthy city like London."

They walked for ten minutes, until they reached the middle of a large, clear space.

"This is excellent. Will you pass the painting, please. I do not imagine you would try and play the fool, but for that very reason I must check."

He handed the painting over. Carefully, using her beautifully manicured nails, she undid the knots and stripped back a corner of the paper.

"It really is superb. How ever he managed it I don't know. There can't be a handful of men in the entire world who would be able to tell this from a Van Dyck."

"Less than that," agreed Verrell, with straight face.

"The man was a genius in his own right. Would you kindly do the parcel up again for me, while I light a cigarette. I would offer you one, but they are scented."

"No, thanks."

"Would you care to know how your companion is?" She watched his face as she flicked her lighter open. Searching for a reaction, she was disappointed.

"I would," he answered calmly.

"She's still very fit. I told her I was coming to meet you and she sent her best regards."

"Tell her I return her good wishes."

"Aren't you interested in knowing when you'll see her next?"

"Of course."

"Then you should show it. Off-hand I would have said you could not have cared less." The cold smile flitted across her features. "As soon as I have checked on this painting she will be free of our gentle captivity." It was a good example of ambiguity.

"You are most considerate."

This time she looked at him sharply, was about to say something, but thought twice. Instead she smoked with the ferocity of a confirmed addict, threw the butt away before it was half finished.

"I'm going," she snapped. "Stay here for the next fifteen minutes. Don't move. Don't bother to watch me leave."

He sat down on the grass. She turned and left, making for the entrance by which he had entered earlier.

He waited the full period, then moved with speed. Outside the park gates he signalled a taxi, gave the address of Wright's office.

IOO

Paula Schmidt was excessively careful. More by nature than because she thought Verrell would try to follow her. He had too much to lose. When almost out of sight, she turned and looked at the seated figure in the open. He was not even bothering to look in her direction. She resumed walking.

The man in park uniform, weeding a flower bed, straightened up.

Outside the gates she turned to the right and walked up Oxford Street.

A shabbily-dressed man with a sandwich-board announcing the end of the world shambled along behind her. The boards were large. They had to be, to conceal the powerful walkie-talkie wireless. A van, belonging to a firm of cleaners, wormed its way through the traffic.

She turned off, past Selfridges, in the direction of Baker Street. The van, unable to go up the 'no entry' road, took the deviation. The driver judged his speed well and reached the main street as she passed, helped by reports from the sandwich-board carrier.

Half-way to Baker Street Station a saloon car stopped. A man, dressed in City clothes, carrying large brief-case and umbrella, got out. He walked along the pavement, stopped, admired a window filled with men's clothing. Paula passed him. He continued on his way, occasionally swinging the umbrella in the air and apparently talking to himself.

The man with the boards turned off.

In a side street was a small Austin car. Paula stepped in and sat in the driving seat. She turned back into the road she had just left, joined the stream of traffic proceeding northwards.

The van drew out from the kerb and followed.

The City gentleman was picked up by the saloon car which made up the leeway and passed the Austin.

They reached the North Circular Road and the saloon tinned right, stopped. Across the road was an old taxi, meter down. It moved off.

The Austin continued straight on until it reached High Road, slowed down as the numbers of the houses reached the thousand, stopped outside a large corner house. The taxi turned down the side road.

A uniformed constable came strolling back towards the main road. Incuriously he watched Paula drive the car into the garage. He continued on his beat.

Verrell had not been long in reaching Wright. The taxi-driver had shown all the signs of a budding grand-prix 'pilote', when a ten-shilling tip was mentioned. He raced up the stairs of the dingy building, entered the glass-fronted doors.

Wright was in his inner sanctum. He stood up. "Good morning. Sit down. Have a cigarette. And for God's sake relieve my curiosity."

"Have you?"

"How did you do it? I've spent hours trying to work it out. I had all the reports in, I've checked and double-checked. For once I really take my hat off to you! Now put me out of my misery. How did you do it?"

"Do what?" Verrell looked as lost as he felt.

"What the hell do you think? Pinch the painting from the Freshman collection, of course."

He laughed. He had to. He laughed so heartily Wright blinked.

"Could you condescend to explain?"

"Here am I worrying about Paula and all you can do is ask stupid questions. Since I didn't pinch it, the answer is I don't know."

"In the circumstances, the least you could do is tell me! I've upset everything to help you out."

"Once again I didn't take that painting."

"Very well." Wright's lips tightened. "If you expect me to believe anyone else in this country could have done that job, you've had it. But if you won't tell me, you won't! I thought you were a better sport, Verrell."

Verrell was about to laugh again, when second thoughts prevailed. Judging by the atmosphere, he should tread softly. "I'm sorry. If I knew how, I'd tell you."

"Skip it."

"Have you still got tracks on the woman?"

"Of course. She's walking down Baker Street."

A man knocked at the door. "Entered a small Austin car, registered number AKN 945, and driven off, sir."

"Which direction?"

"The same, sir."

Wright stood up and walked across to a wall-sized map. "My guess is Barnet way. Want to get moving, Verrell?" "What do you suggest?"

"Down the back you'll find a car. It's fast. The wireless is tuned to pick us up. We'll let you know what's happening as you go along. Anything else we can do?"

"Thanks a lot, but you've worked wonders already. I'll buy you a rehoboam of champagne when it's all over."

"I'd rather hear how you did the "

"I didn't."

Wright mastered himself. "I don't know what all this is about. But are you certain it isn't too big for one man? You can have some of my chaps if you want."

"Again, thanks, but I'll play it alone."

"As you wish. The car's below," he ended abruptly. Wright watched the other leave. By God, he thought viciously, they'd better watch out if they try the rough stuff on him. I'll see they get something a darned sight rougher. But the blighter might have told me!

Verrell raced below, started the car. He switched the wireless on. Not until he was a mile from the office did the faint crackling give way to a message.

"Party continuing along same road. George one and George two both in contact."

As soon as that message was completed, Wright was on the air explaining to him what it meant.

He drove with fiendish brilliance, using every ounce of the car's power, heedless of the other traffic. A rain of curses followed his wake as taxi-drivers were deprived of space they themselves were about to squeeze into; or near-learners saw a car race past them with inches only to spare.

By the time Paula had parked her car in the garage he was seven minutes behind. Seven minutes by her rate of progress that was. He did it in five.

There was no time for a prepared campaign. Or for making the slightest check. He just parked the car, walked along the side road until he came to the side entrance to the house. The door opened as he turned the handle. Nobody had even bothered to lock it.

The kitchen, the first room he came to, was deserted. Not until he was in the hall did he hear the faint sound of conversation behind one of the two doors to the right of the corridor. He distinguished the voice of Paula, and that of a man.

He passed the door, came to the foot of the steep staircase. Step by step he ascended. The wood was not covered by a carpet, and despite every care he took, one step creaked loudly as he gently shifted his weight on to it. He remained poised for instant movement. But nothing happened.

On the landing were five doors. The first two were bathroom and bedroom, opened as he turned the handle. The next one was locked. He put his ear to the door panel. Faintly he managed to pick up the sound of someone breathing.

The lock was more complicated than he expected. None of his keys would turn it immediately, the nearest fit only took the tumblers half-way. He took a pencil and scratched some of the carbon on to the key. The second time he used the key, the imprint in the carbon showed which parts needed filing. Round his waist was his belt of tools. He took out of it a file, started work.

In seven minutes he had the door open. Diana was a sorry sight. Usually immaculate from groomed head of hair to handmade shoes, lying on the bed she looked as though she were recovering from a world-beater of a hang-over. Her hair was a rumpled mass of knotted ends; her blouse was stained and shapeless. Her pencil-slim skirt, dragged up over her knees, might have been a black sack hurriedly thrown over her to maintain some modesty.

It was an old-fashioned bed, with iron headrest and foot rail. One pair of handcuffs lashed her left arm to the top, one pair her right foot to the rail. Stretched as she was, it was impossible to turn and twist more than a few inches.

He removed the gag — a rag, secured by a handkerchief.

"It's about time," she said. Her throat worked at the effort of speaking.

"Sorry I'm a bit late," he replied. "Got held up in the rain."

He undid the handcuffs with a small instrument shaped like a pick. Then gently helped her to sit up, taking part of her weight on his shoulder.

"Could you get me a glass of water?" she whispered.

In the bathroom he filled a tooth-mug with water, careful that the tap was not turned on sufficiently to send a rushing noise through the pipes.

Diana watched him return with eagerness. She drank the water with the care usually reserved for vintage wines.

"Is that better! Richard, where is?"

"Downstairs."

"She's foul, Richard. I've never met anyone so vile." With an effort she controlled herself. "I'd almost begun to give up hope."

"What — knowing I was around? Shame on you." He smiled.

Diana relaxed. There was something extra special about that smile.

"Stay right here, and take this." He handed her a revolver. For once in his life he had carried a gun... with Diana in mind. "If either of them comes up, shoot first. Then ask them what they want. Use both hands and rest the gun on something. Aim for the stomach."

"What are you going to do?"

"I..." He grinned without humour. "I'm all set for a little chat about politics. Be seeing you!"

One moment he was there. The next he had gone. Diana gripped the gun tight. It would be a personal pleasure if Paula should walk in.

Verrell reached the foot of the stairs, advanced to the second door. Close to, he could hear what was being said, but his slightly rusty German had to work overtime.

"I tell you there's nothing here." It was the man speaking.

"There must be. He wouldn't be such a fool as to try and get away with that."

"Never mind what he's tried. There's nothing here. Look for yourself."

"But it's one of the paintings."

"Is it? Suppose it's a genuine Van Dyck?"

"And where would he get one from? You're talking rubbish, Carl."

"Rubbish or not, you've made a mess of things. The painting in the Freshman collection was one of the Bassetes which came from von Steiner's collection. It had the paper in it. It's not here, Paula. You've been taken for a fool."

"If I have, the little idiot upstairs will suffer."

"How does that help us? By all means go and amuse yourself, but try and remember we want that painting/*

"Am I likely to forget it? Ring up that young man, Verrell, and ask him to listen-in while I start work on the girl. I'll guarantee she makes enough noise. It will convince him."

"And if it doesn't?"

"Worry about that later. He'll play our game when he's listened for a minute or two. My hands have not lost their cunning."

"Very well, go ahead."

Paula rose from her chair. Before she could reach the door it opened.

Verrell stepped inside. "Going somewhere?" he asked, pleasantly.

For a moment the two could not believe their senses. The man recovered himself first. He started to reach for his right-hand pocket.

"I shouldn't," said Verrel, calmly.

His cold insolence held them. Carl let his hand fall to his side.

"Who...?"

"Ask Smithy over there — looking remarkably unpleasant at the moment."

"Verrell," muttered the woman tonelessly. Her mouth was a thin, hard streak of red.

"Idiot!" snapped Carl. "Fool! I warned you. He followed you here."

"He can't have done. I'll swear it. I took every possible precaution," she mumbled.

"You'll swear it! How else do you think he got here?"

"To stop this argument developing any further," broke in Verrell softly, "the answer is that your suggestion is quite correct. Little Paula showed me the way home."

"You liar. You filthy liar."

"What a nasty thing to say," he complained.

"I left you in the park. It was impossible for you to follow me."

"I can fly!"

"Swine!" muttered Paula. The one word expressed her feelings. It also indicated what she wanted to do to the smiling man standing carelessly in the centre of the room.

"Now, to keep the records straight, it's my turn." There was a harsh snap in Verreirs voice. "Who's this — the missing Mr. Jackson?"

The man's glare was sufficient answer.

"The gentleman who's just lost his wife. You don't look so bereaved as you should."

"She was not my wife. It was your big mistake."

"Didn't matter, did it?"

"You think yourself too clever," he sneered. "I took advantage of the mistake and won! It did matter, Mr. Cocky Verrell."

"Who was the murdered woman?"

"You still haven't discovered?" he sneered. "Your wits need sharpening. I'll tell you. She was our maid in Germany."

"I thought she might be."

"You thought! Do you expect me to believe that? When you do not know who I am?"

"Come, Mr. Carl Schmidt, you underestimate your popularity."

That his guess had been justified soon became apparent to Verrell. He cut across the flow of swear-words.

"You were in charge of a concentration camp… job runs in the family. Your record is nearly, but not quite, as bad as your wife's. All this meant that at the end of the war the two of you had to vanish, quickly." Verrell was watching the other's face closely. To know the moment his guesswork became wrong.

"So?"

"So you and your wife became Austrian refugees — rich refugees. But as a couple you were too well known. The long and the short of it. You, tall and fat. Your wife, small, dainty, looking like an angel."

Paula was, by no stretch of the imagination, looking like an angel just then.

"The whole of the Allied forces were looking for you. Not to mention relatives of the people you'd liquidated. So you changed your wife for a stodgy uneducated maid. And vice versa. It was enough."

"You know a lot," snarled Carl. "How did you know who my wife was?"

"She told me."

"Imbecile," he yelled at Paula. "Now you proclaim the fact from every roof-top."

"What does it matter?" A quick signal passed between them. "I wanted him to know what the girl was in for."

"Why did you die?" Verrell asked.

"Because you played your hand so stupidly. You wanted a discreet silence. In case someone else started thinking before you had all five paintings. My wife would collect mine from the bank — after she had identified the body as mine at your orders. Once that was done I was out of the way and no one remembered the Bassete. And all this time you had me to work on... You'll regret what you did then."

"Did it hurt?" he asked curiously.

Carl swore again. "And all the time you said how clever you'd been. Using my wife as a hostage for my good behaviour. Imagine how I laughed. You could kill the maid fifty times over as far as I was concerned."

"Certainly got tangled up," remarked Verrell. "You disappeared via a dead body — unwillingly. You escaped, and of course weren't worried that you were officially dead. That end of things didn't matter to you. So you turn up and collect the Bassete. In consequence your maid-wife is murdered."

"Maybe now you see why your stupid mistake mattered," sneered the other. "If you had taken Paula in the first instance. Or if you had said you would kill her if I refused to talk... things would have been different. I would not like anything to happen to her."

"If I had Paula for a wife," remarked Verrell calmly and dispassionately, "I'd be only too thankful if someone would offer to remove her free of charge."

Her face contorted with rage. "That was an unwise thing to say."

"In fact I'd donate a small offering."

She stared at him with an expression which would have jolted the Gorgon's head.

He grinned. "Just before I go, I'd better remove that bit of paper from the table."

Before the other two realized what he was doing, Verrell reached across the table and picked up a small square of paper, similar to the one he had found in the Bassete painting. He put it in his top pocket. Smiled. Turned to go.

Chapter Eleven

Schmidt started to move.

"Don't bother to see me out," smiled Verrell. "And many thanks for having this paper ready for me. I was afraid I'd have to ask you where the painting was you'd taken from the bank."

"Carl!" snapped the woman.

Her husband responded, threw off the strange bemusement brought about by the calm, unarmed Verrell. He had an automatic in his coat pocket. He tried to reach it with his right hand.

Verrell had chosen his own ground with care. At his side was a heavy glass ash-tray. With one motion he scooped it up, threw it hard at the man, followed it by hurling himself across the space.

The gun was half out of the pocket when the glass piece crashed into Carl's face. He howled with the suddenness of the pain. Then his right arm was caught and forced upwards and backwards until he had to suffer a broken arm, or drop the automatic. He dropped it.

Verrell kicked the gun to one side, released the arm-lock.

Paused. Waited for the heavier German to rush him. He was not disappointed. Carl lurched forward, arms outstretched.

Verrell half turned as their bodies met. He wrapped his right hand round the other's waist, caught the left hand in his own, allowed the momentum of the rush to bear him over slightly. At that point he pulled down with his left hand, kicked up with his foot, thrust upwards with his whole body. Carl was airborne for a short distance. Then he smashed into a wooden chair.

Before the German could recover his full senses Verrell brought him upright by the simple measure of pulling his hair. He then kicked away his feet and let go of the hair. Carl slapped the floor with painful intensity.

Still there was a little fight left. Until Verrell pulled the other on top of him as he deliberately fell backwards on to the floor, and used his foot as heavy leverage. This time the wall suffered. Carl remained crumpled up on the floor.

As Verrell picked himself up from the floor he received a smashing blow on his shoulder, meant for his head but avoided by some sixth sense. Paula aimed another blow with the chair-leg, missing as he rolled to one side.

She dropped the wooden club and raced to the far corner by the door. As she stood erect she held the automatic in her hand.

"You'll regret your impetuosity," she mouthed, unable to speak clearly for the rage which made her shake.

Verrell rubbed his shoulder and arm and had no illusions about the truth of the saying that the female was more deadly than the male.

The three of them had forgotten Diana. As Paula was about to fire, a sudden sound behind made her half turn. It was too late. The blow was unscientific, but effective, coming as it did at the base of the neck.

"Nothing has ever given me greater pleasure," said Diana with pure bliss in her voice. She watched the other woman slump to the floor, lowered the revolver with which she had delivered the coup de grace.

He grinned. "Not a lady-like sentiment."

"But something to tell the grandchildren about." Then she sat down. The sudden surge of energy departed leaving her still weak.

"Before I forget it — my thanks! Anytime you want a glowing testimonial just call on me. 'Strong woman, expert with butt-ends of guns. Silence any argument.' "

"I'll remember that. I heard such a frightful din I thought it was about time I came and gave a hand. Despite your explicit instructions."

"I'll add first-class initiative."

"Richard, have you got a cigarette on you? I've been wanting one for I don't know how long."

He brought his case out of his pocket and offered it.

She inhaled deeply and gratefully. "Tell me — just how the deuce did you manage to find me? Telepathy?"

"A little luck and a lot of help," he answered. "Traced you through friend Paula. She wanted something from me. Which reminds me, I might as well wrap it up."

He crossed the room, picked up the Van Dyck which had been removed from its frame.

no

"Is that all you have to say?"

"There's not much else," he answered innocently.

"What did the police have to say?"

"The police..." He bent over his task, trying to find an answer.

Diana chuckled. "That's bad. The police have no idea that a well-known young woman was abducted and threatened with lots of nasty things. I must say, Richard, you've got a nerve. It's a wonder my father hasn't started asking questions in the House."

"He did ring me up just before I left this morning." "Wanting to know where I'd got to, I suppose. And why I wasn't in when he rang last night. What did you say?"

"Roberts said I was out."

She looked at him demurely. "I can't quite make up my mind what to tell him. Best thing I can think of is to say I've been with you all the time."

"You can't do that," he protested.

"Why not? He rather likes youl" Then she took pity on him. "Don't worry, I won't."

He eased a finger round a collar that had suddenly become tight. He changed the conversation — hopefully. "When did these beauties pick you up?"

"The moment you'd left me. Hadn't taken my coat off when the bell rang. Naturally I thought it was you, forgotten something. I opened the door, and the next thing I knew was that I was being bundled into the back of a car as though I were a sack of potatoes. We arrived here and Paula regaled me with her past history. Ugh!"

"Mentioning which," he said, "Paula is back in the world of the living, and Carl won't be long." He looked at the man lying on the ground, laughed. "I feel we ought to leave our visiting-card. Got a pair of scissors on you?"

"No. Why?"

"You'll see. There should be a pair somewhere in the house. Would you be up to having a quick look?"

She smiled. "I'm on my way. How will you have them, large or small?"

"As they come."

Diana went out. Paula was sufficiently conscious to reach with her hand to the back of her neck and feel the spot which had received such a solid blow. She winced.

"Not too bad, I hope?" he enquired kindly.

"You damn well know it is," she snapped.

"Aspirins are what you need. Or Veganin. Take a couple before it gets really painful."

"We'll kill you for this."

He grinned. "Thought you wouldn't be wishing me a happy birthday."

106

Diana returned. "Success! Found these in the kitchen." She held up a large pair of scissors.

"Good. Just what the doctor ordered. If you'll give them to me I can satisfy a lifelong ambition."

Carl Schmidt was back in circulation. Verrell had thought him still incapable of movement. Realized he was wrong when the other made a lunge forward. The sight of the scissors had awakened too many memories for Carl to remain quiet. But it was a wasted effort. All strength had drained from his body and he collapsed after a couple of paces.

"They certainly breed your type with thick skulls," remarked Verrell, as he advanced across the room. He moved until he was at the back of Carl, fixed the scissors on his right hand. Just before he began, he checked on Paula.

"Keep an eye on her, will you, Diana? She should be nice and quiet. But just in case."

"Don't worry, Richard, she won't move. This shoe of mine has a very solid heel to it."

Satisfied, he wasted no more time. He worked rapidly and unskilfully. In three minutes he stood back and admired his work.

He had cut Carl's hair as closely as was possible. That was except for a ridge in the centre of the head which extended from back to front. An electric pair of clippers could hardly have gone closer.

Diana was delighted. "Wild man from Borneo isn't in the same class."

"Thank you." He bowed ironically. "I think I've been too lenient. At one time I thought of going over the whole scalp with a razor. Would have made him jump!"

"I think we've missed something."

"Don't be so bloodthirsty! Are you ready to go, now? If we stay any longer we may become unpopular."

"After you've handed those scissors over."

"Why?" Then he understood. "You can't…"

"No?"

Paula made far more fuss than her husband. She had nicer hair.

"Just like a boiled egg," said Diana, unkindly. "You'll need lots of new hats; none of the old ones will fit."

Paula choked as the words cascaded one into the other. Helpless, she had been robbed of her glorious hair. Tears of mortification sprang into her eyes.

Deep in self-pity she was not conscious of the precise moment the two left the house. Stopping for lack of breath, she became aware that she and her husband were alone. All shaven and shorn.

"You hopeless idiot," she snarled.

"You, you brainless half-wit," he retorted. "You led him here."

The row was long and furious.

Diana admitted she wanted a good strong drink, but, woman-like, refused to think of it until she had been to her flat and bathed, changed, and made up Returning to the centre of London, Verrell drove gently, as though making up for the havoc he had caused on the outward run.

"May I give you a spot of very strong advice?"

"Of course, Richard."

"Move into a hotel, or stay with friends. But whatever you do, don't go back to your flat for the next few nights. Paula won't waste any time trying to get her claws into you again."

"Good understatement." She shivered. "Could you run me round to a hotel after I've collected some things from the flat?"

"Of course."

"Thanks. Believe me, I shan't move into dark and unfrequented by-ways. As for father's guests…! They'll have to get along without me."

"Ill keep in touch with you."

'Try not doing so and see what happens." The rest of the day was uneventful.

As soon as he was back in the peace of his own study Verrell took from his wallet the compressed roll of tissue-paper which he had taken from the Schmidts. What fresh light would this piece throw on the mystery of the forged paintings? He opened it out, smoothed the creases, eagerly inspected it…

It couldn't be. His brain was playing a trick upon him. Or were his eyes to blame? No, it couldn't be…

But it was. The second roll of tissue was identical with the first. The same shape, the same size, the same two figures: 52, the same two corners missing…

No, not the same comers, by George! He opened his safe, extracted from it the tissue he had taken from the frame of the museum Bassete. He placed it on the desk beside the one Schmidt had guarded with such care. With one exception the two rolls were identical, but whereas the first was minus its two upper comers, the second had lost its lower corners.

That there was probably a reason for the corners to be missing was obvious. But what was it?

Two hours later he stopped puzzling, feeling that he was no nearer to solving the mystery. In spite of this he smiled happily, for two facts emerged from his study of the two tissues: one, that the mystery was probably to be solved only when all five pieces of paper had been assembled (if there were five, as he began to assume); and two, that if he couldn't make any headway in locating the stolen loot, nor could the other two parties. In fact, it was beginning to seem that there was still time and a chance for him to be in at the kill — or even to make the kill!

He was enjoying his after-breakfast cigarette the following morning when the front-door bell rang. Roberts left the room, but soon returned.

"A Mr. Phipson would like to speak to you, sir."

"What's he want?" The name was new.

"He didn't say, sir. Just that he would like to speak to you for a moment."

"Has he got any hair?"

"Yes, sir." Roberts betrayed supreme lack of surprise at the question.

"Ask him to come in. Check in a minute if he would like some coffee."

"Yes, sir."

Mr. Phipson walked in. Said good morning in an excessively warm tone of voice. Accepted the seat offered him, then showed difficulty in proceeding further.

Verrell knew him better as Parson.

"I have come, Mr. Verrell, to make you a proposition." He stopped, offered cigarettes.

"Sounds interesting! But for the moment I'm afraid I can't place you. I really have an appalling memory for faces and names. Never can connect the two."

"We haven't met before."

"Forgive me. From the way you talked I thought we had."

Parson drew heavily on his cigarette. He did not like the smiling man opposite. Nor the way he was treating the meeting. There was more than a hint of latent strength, allied with a trace of mocking humour. It upset him. To say nothing of the fact that Sam and Jim had left the flat after their visit in a vastly different state to that in which they'd entered it.

"I'm sorry," he said after a pause. He was not quite certain what he was apologizing for. "I thought you might like to hear what I have to say."

"Of course. That's why I'm listening."

109

Roberts knocked, entered, made certain there was no trouble. He asked the guest if he would like some coffee.

"No thanks," muttered Parson nervously, "I've just had some."

"What do you want?" asked Verrell, when they were alone.

The other took the plunge. "You've been staying at the Freshman house."

"Well?"

"You're friendly with Diana Freshman."

"You're becoming insolent." Verrell still spoke good-humouredly.

"I…" he gulped. "A painting was stolen from the collection, wasn't it?"

"I believe so."

"You displayed a remarkable interest in the affair." "Really."

"Other paintings have been stolen lately. Paintings by the same person. You know whom I mean?"

"No," said Verrell, "tell me."

"Look here, Mr. Verrell," muttered Parson, "I'm not here to crack jokes."

"Then you really have something of interest to say. Might we gradually find out what it is?" He smiled.

"All right. One was pinched from the Old Masters' Gallery. We… I want it."

"I expect the museum does too."

"I'll pay you damned well for it. A cool thousand."

"For what?"

"For this painting. The one I've just blasted well been talking about." Parson was speaking roughly. Upset by the fact that he was completely unable to gauge the man to whom he was talking. He wished the hell someone else could have been given the job.

Verrell answered deceptively smoothly. "That's a lot of money for something which is, I believe, called hot. Incidentally, what makes you think I have it?"

"All right, be ruddy clever. You weren't poking round that museum day after day for nothing. I've given you a fair offer. What the hell have you got to say about it?"

Verrell looked faintly surprised. "You're very impetuous." "Look — I said a thousand. We'll have that painting. So don't hang on too long. To make your mind up… two thousand. One-pound notes. Or, if you prefer it… I can promise you a bullet where it hurts." Parson realized his threat carried no weight. How could it? When he was scared stiff of the man in front of him.

"Funny you should mention that," Verrell remarked lazily. "Strange thing happened the other day. Someone took a pot-shot at me. I want to meet the marksman." In a dreamy fashion he looked directly at the other.

Parson shivered. "Next time you might not escape so easily/' he managed.

"Or the marksman?"

In desperation the other jerked their conversation back to where they were. "How about this two thousand?"

"Of course. We were discussing a proposition. Two thousand pounds in cash for a painting I haven't got. What a pity! I do hate missing chances."

"Does that mean the answer's no?"

"You're very quick on the uptake."

"You don't want to reconsider?"

"I was trying to give that impression."

Parson played his last trump. At least he'd been told it was a trump. "You wouldn't like anything to happen to Diana Freshman?"

Verrell laughed. The Schmidts were way ahead on that line. "Think it might?" he asked softly.

The other saw the danger signals. It was lucky for him he had taken two double brandies just before his visit. "Yes."

"Then a last word. Forget it. I don't like you very much. Only as an object of curiosity. I should like you still less if anything should happen to her." His voice was icy. "Should anything happen to her, Mr. Parson... or was it Phipson...? I shall come along and find you, and snap your rotten neck in two." He leaned back in the chair and smiled.

"Look here, I..."

"You were about to say?"

He gulped. "Nothing."

"You want your hat before you leave." Verrell called for Roberts.

"Yes, sir."

"See this gentleman out, please."

Roberts handed Parson his hat, showed him to the front door. From the small window he could see when the caller reached the pavement. As soon as that happened he followed.

At the corner Parson turned and checked that he was not being followed. Roberts had been expecting that move. He had, himself, turned and retraced his steps thirty seconds before, thus presenting only an anonymous back. In his small hand-mirror he watched his man turn the corner.

There was little difficulty in following the other while they were in comparatively quiet streets. But once they reached Marble Arch it became a hectic task. Twice sudden eddies of people almost made him lose contact. He shortened the distance between them.

Five minutes later Parson waved his arm vigorously. A taxi stopped. He entered. Roberts checked, but there was no other taxi in sight. He shrugged his shoulders and returned to the flat.

Parson drove to a house in Swiss Cottage. He felt slightly sick. Carr was the kind of man he would like to be. Clever, ruthless, successful. He also had a vicious temper. Lately it had been more and more in evidence. It was likely to appear again when Parson made his report.

Strangely, Carr listened to the slightly fictitious report without any signs of anger.

"In other words you made a botch of it," he stated baldly. "This bloke has got you all bewitched. Thank God I'm free now to look after him myself. But first things first. One of the boys has found him."

"Who?"

"Jackson, of course. The fellow we've been trying to find for weeks. Not much wonder things go wrong with people as dumb as you around! I was willing to bet a packet he'd make for London. Sure enough he did. As soon as Jim gets back we'll go have a word with him."

"That's good work."

Carr ignored the inferred compliment. He pulled a bottle of whisky across the table, poured himself out a drink. "Here, have one. Might put some guts into you."

"Cheers."

He grunted in reply. "When we've collected from him there's only Verrell. Had the devil's own luck so far, but he's reached the end of the line." He was talking to himself more than to the other. "This time tomorrow we'll be ready to move. In a couple of days we'll have cleaned up. And the way prices have sky-rocketed we should make a cool half-million at the very lowest."

"Pounds?" Parson leaned forward and licked his lips. It 118

was the first time he had heard a figure of that size mentioned.

"No, pence/' snapped Carr sarcastically. "What the hell do you keep in that head of yours?"

"Well, I…"

"Forget the explanations."

"Where are we selling the stuff?"

"Over the other side. Contacts all fixed up. We get a better price and don't have to worry about bringing the stuff over here."

Carr did not go on to explain the rest of his plans. Which included the fact that Parson would not be sharing in the 'cool half-million'.

Jim returned.

"Right, let's go."

The three men left in a car which had not yet been missed by its owner. They reached the house, parked.

Carr rang the bell. The door was opened by Carl, who made the fatal mistake of hesitating.

"Nice to see you again." Carr slammed the door open, walked in, closely followed by the others.

"What do you want?" Carl looked at the two guns covering him. He cursed himself.

"A chat."

Carr checked that the first room to the right was empty. "Bring him in here. Jim, check the rest of the house."

Parson kept his gun in Carl's back as they entered.

"Just going out?" asked Carr, noticing the cap the other was wearing. "We were just in time." He pulled the cap off. The sight made him roar with laughter. "Pukka Prussian hair-cut."

In the short ensuing silence they heard steps approach. Carr moved back into the hall and waited. The door opened, Paula entered.

He grabbed her by her shoulders and forced her into the room.

"Not a bad bag," he drawled.

She spoke rapidly in German.

"Shut up."

Jim returned. "House is empty."

"All right. Make yourself useful. Keep an eye on this woman while I have a word with Carl."

Carr moved forward two paces. He grinned sardonically. "You've got something I want."

"Havel?"

"Where is it?"

"You tell me."

"I'm doing the asking."

"So it seems."

"Where's that painting? And what came out of it?"

"I have no idea."

"Last chance to talk."

Carl spat.

It took a long time to break his resistance. And by the end Carr had used up all the tricks he knew.

"You still say Verrell took it from you?"

"Yes." It was a croak.

"Damn!" Carr stared at the floor for a moment. Then he took a gun out of his pocket. "I've been wanting to do this for a long, long time."

Casually he pulled the trigger three times. The silencer dimmed most of the noise.

Paula had been all but forgotten. Jim was supposed to be guarding her, but his attention had been centred on Carl. She chose her moment with care. Her foot slammed up and caught the man behind her in the groin. He slumped to the floor with a single bellow of pain.

She was out of the room before the others had time to overcome their surprise.

Carr fired once. But only as a gesture. "Fool," he snapped.

Jim could hardly speak as the searing pain seemed to grow in intensity.

"We'd better get out," suggested Parson nervously.

"Stop shaking."

Jim pulled himself up off the floor.

"You..." Carr stopped short. It was not the time to tell Jim a few home truths. "Come on, get the hell out of here. Time to start thinking about Verrell. By God, he'll wish he never stuck his nose into this!"

Chapter Twelve

Wright arrived just as Verrell was finishing lunch. Roberts scarcely had time to announce him before he brushed past.

"Glad to find you in. Rather gathered you weren't working these days."

"Have you eaten?"

"Yes. If you count sandwiches and a cup of dishwater as a meal."

"How about a cup of real coffee, to take away the taste? And a liqueur?"

"Just what the doctor ordered," Wright agreed with decision. "And if you think I have a conscience about accepting anything that is offered to me in this flat…" He spotted a box of cigarettes on the table. "Good. Decent ones, for a change." He helped himself. "Books still doing well?"

"So, so. Can't complain."

"Met someone the other day who told me to buy one of yours." He blew out a cloud of smoke and sighed his satisfaction. "If I can remember the title you can do the decent thing."

"Autographed?"

"Why not, if it adds to its monetary value?"

Verrell chuckled. "As complimentary as ever! Which poison?"

"Brandy, if you have it. And while you are pouring it out you can tell me about things."

He moved over to the cocktail-cabinet, and poured out two glasses of Remy, Martin. "Things?" he enquired.

Wright made a gesture of hopeless resignation. "For one whole morning a considerable portion of my entire department was disrupted on your behalf. Remember?"

"Yes."

"And you ask me, what things? That's what I want to know. What was going on?"

"Quite a lot in a quiet way. Abduction, robbery, grievous bodily harm, and, if I hadn't turned up, probably a spot of murder." He passed over the brandy, sat down.

"Cheers," said Wright before smelling the bouquet of the brandy, then sipping it. He leaned back, relaxed and contented. "What was at the back of it all?"

"I don't really know."

"You don't say! Disposes of everything with indecent haste. Do you expect me to believe you? Suppose I try again. What started everything?"

"You wouldn't want me to lie, would you?" This in a most innocent voice.

Wright snorted.

"Then you'll just have to accept the truth. I don't know." "What brought you into the business?"

"Trying to solve an impossibility."

Wright glanced up at the ceiling. "Damned if I know why I put up with you. A word from me would see you in gaol quicker than you could say Jack Robinson."

"Have another brandy?" Verrell suggested. "Put you in a kindlier mood."

Wright snorted, and obligingly finished his brandy.

"Every time you go anywhere I spend days clearing up the mess," he continued. "Why did you say *probably* a spot of murder? You know there was a body at the house we checked your woman to."

"What!" Verrell relaxed, chuckled. "You're pulling my leg. I'll buy it."

"Innocence personified," the other man jeered. He grew sterner. "Come on, Mr. Verrell, how about it?"

"There *was* a murder?"

"Yes."

"Man or woman?"

Wright's cold blue eyes stared at his host. "If I didn't know too damn well it wasn't your doing "

"Man or woman?" Verrell insisted.

"A corpse. Male."

"Yes, of course "

"I mean, that a corpse was murdered. In other words, the victim has been identified as a man who was killed some time back, in a car accident. You see, in these days a man has to die twice before he's really dead," Wright finished heavily.

Verrell grinned. Wright was always at his best when he was most lugubrious.

"Man of the name of Jackson," he added. "Maybe." •

"Try Schmidt/'

Wright sat up. "German?"

"Remember that concentration camp in Northern France with a reputation for advanced brutality?"

Wright's expression sharpened. "So that was our friend the corpse! Then he's no loss to the world. By the way, he was given rather hectic treatment before he was shot." He paused. "Then who was killed in the accident?"

"Ask me another."

"So I would, and plenty more, if I thought you would answer them." He went into a reverie. "Big stakes!" he muttered.

Verrell waited. All too well he knew the other man's extraordinary deductive reasoning. He wouldn't be at all surprised, he told himself, if Wright produced the right answers.

"This is damn' good brandy," Wright volunteered. "I'll know where to come when I want some more."

"That's a date."

"Was Schmidt alive when you left the house?"

"Very much so, though a trifle shaken-up perhaps."

Wright smiled; something he did not do very often. "So I surmised. You know, it's not the first time you've left someone a trifle shaken-up. You must have a serviceable right hook."

"Serviceable," Verrell agreed.

"You're providing me with quite a few riddles."

"Solvable?"

"What man obscures, man can solve. Or isn't that quite what I mean? You're the literary one."

"Thanks for the compliment. I write only thrillers so I'm not literary. Another cigarette?"

"Thanks." Wright glanced at his watch. "Time I was moving. If I stay away from things for more than a minute or two, heaven alone knows what I find. Don't forget that champagne you promised me," he added abruptly.

"First I have to find the rehoboam."

"I'll give you the address of a wineshop that has several."

Verrell grimaced as Wright left with his usual abruptness. He was frankly puzzled. What had the visit signified? Wright had not demanded a full explanation, but had been content to be fobbed off; which was totally unlike him. That could mean only one thing: that he already had a vague hint of what was happening, gleaned no doubt from scraps of information which had filtered through to him. And he had come to have that suspicion confirmed or denied.

Had he said anything which might have given Wright a lead? Verrell wondered. He thought back on the few sentences that had been spoken. His first reaction was that everything had been so vague nothing much of importance could possibly have been gleaned. And yet...

Wasting no more time on surmises he transferred his thoughts to another aspect of the present situation. That of staying whole and unharmed. Paula Schmidt would now, more than ever, desire his death — but not, presumably, so long as he retained possession of any of the missing (missing as far as she was concerned) squares. Parson and friends were in the same predicament. Between the contending parties life held out the prospect of being extremely lively for some time to come.

Either side, he concluded, would hope and plan to obtain his body and person, with a view to 'persuading1 him to be more co-operative. Or, perhaps more likely, they would try to use Diana — as Paula had already done, and Parson had threatened to do — as a hostage. Whichever might be their choice — and who could say that both courses would not be followed? — it was obvious that all precautions would have to be taken in order not to play into their hands.

One focal point was, undoubtedly, his flat. Parson's men had already found their way in once. It was feasible to anticipate that they would try a second time. He rang for Roberts.

"Could you arrange to sleep here for a few nights?"

Roberts's reply was prompt. "Yes, sir."

"Good. Then be a good chap and do that, so that you can keep an eye on the place if I'm not here. Know anything about electricity?" He was sure that the question was a safe one. Roberts was quite a handyman.

"Something, sir."

"In that case you might get weaving, and fit all doors and windows up with some sort of an alarm."

The valet's face didn't even twitch. "May I take it that you are expecting uninvited guests, sir?"

"You may. And they won't be policemen. I hope," he added piously. "Also, do something about the gates in the 124

yard, and fix some sort of an identification on the street door so that well know who is using a key."

The imperturbable Roberts nodded agreement, and then went on to suggest other arrangements which would go far to confound the unwanted.

Verrell gave him a free hand, so he left the room to begin his task without a moment's delay.

Two more things remained to be done. First, to 'phone Diana, to make sure she was still in good health and spirits.

"Richard!" She failed to conceal the note of pleasure in her voice. "Here have I been stewing for goodness knows how long, waiting to hear from you, and only now do you condescend to ring me up."

He chuckled. "You forget I'm a working man." "Nonsense." She obviously did not believe that one had to work when one was a writer. "Now, another time…" They talked for nearly ten minutes before he rang off, satisfied that she was taking seriously the precautions he outlined.

The second job was to 'phone Wright. But he was out, and not likely to be back in his office for several hours. Verrell wondered whether Wright's outing had anything to do with himself. Could be, he reflected. A wily old fox.

Thinking of Wright brought back the memory of something the other man had said not long since. "What man obscures, man can solve." In other words, no problem was too tough to be cracked. If man had spirited away the painting from the Freshman collection, then man should be able to find out how the incredible feat was performed.

How far had he, Verrell, got in breaking down the mystery? That question was an easy one to answer. Nowhere! Why had he got nowhere? Had he missed something of importance; the only item that might make the entire set-up plain? Or was he looking at the problem from the wrong angle, as it were?

He checked through the items in the theft, one by one. A man had entered the exhibition hall and stolen the painting. In doing so he had set off the alarm, and brought into action the machinery which would prevent his escape. These were the facts in a nutshell. Simple, plain unvarnished facts. Except in one respect. The man *had* escaped!

After he had thought along these lines for several minutes he realized, for the first time, that he had mentally followed, in his reasoning, the sequence of events, as they had happened; a sequence which always led to the one invariable solution, that the theft was impossible. In short, he had been trying to prove the impossible possible.

What was needed was a touch of Chestertonian philosophy. As an exponent and practitioner of the literal, when Chesterton made a character refer to a man as living in The Firs1 on such and such Common, he meant precisely that — no more and no less. He meant, a house built in a fir-tree. A literal translation.

Now, a literal interpretation of the present facts proved that the theft was impossible. Impossible from the moment that the thief had passed through the swing doors into the exhibition. It followed, therefore, that if something could not have happened, it had not happened. The painting had not been stolen.

But the painting had been stolen. That was a concrete fact that nothing could disprove. It was no longer hanging in its proper place on the wall, it was nowhere else in the exhibition, it was missing.

Had it been taken off the wall while the mysterious stranger was still in the exhibition? It couldn't have been, for otherwise he would have been caught like a rat in a trap. Yet when a search was made of the place, after the steel shutters had been raised, no stranger was found. If no stranger was to be found, then no stranger could have entered the room containing the missing picture. If no stranger entered the room, then no painting could have disappeared.

But the painting had disappeared. Yet when the alarm was set off, this must have been at a moment when the exhibition hall was empty. *Ergo*: the theft of the picture and the setting off of the alarm were not simultaneous!

He reached for a cigarette, lit it. He knew his thoughts were too excited for clear reasoning, so he deliberately paused to give his seething imagination time to catch up with itself, as it were. Very soon he was asking himself more questions.

If the theft and the alarm were not simultaneous, why not? How had the picture been removed without setting off the alarm? For seconds the answer eluded him, then it became clear. The alarm did not sound because the electricity was cut off! No, not switched off, because all the switches were in the 126

main building. Besides, nothing had been said of any current failure. And even if there had been a cut in the electricity supply, the private plant would have automatically cut in, thus ensuring a continuous current. The lights had remained on, but the alarm had failed. Why? How? The *cable* connecting the alarm, which was coupled with the machinery for dropping the shutters, had been cut.

What, finally, had set off the alarm? Answers were becoming simplified. The restoration of the circuit after the picture had been stolen and transferred elsewhere.

He now had a mysterious someone who had cut the alarm cable, removed the Bassete from its usual position, transferred the picture elsewhere, and then re-joined the cable, thus setting off the alarm. No wonder the room was empty when searched!

The next problem was one of timing. How long had the painting been missing? Not for long, for evidence had shown that the Bassete had been on the wall less than thirty minutes before the alarm had sounded. Thirty minutes, or less? In that period who had visited the collection, or been in the west wing? Only the mysterious stranger and the two guards.

If there had been no theft at the time when the alarm was set off, might one not assume that there had been no stranger? If there were no stranger, then the guards themselves were the guilty parties. They alone had given a description of the stranger; they alone had been in the west wing.

The guards? Or one guard? Each had lent substance to the illusory man by describing him, but powers of suggestion are amazingly effective; it was possible that one of the guards had planted a description of the alleged stranger in the mind of the other.

Which guard was the guilty man, if only one were guilty? Johns or Trapes? Probably Johns, who was nearest to the collection, for Trapes was looking for the packet of cigarettes which he had left in his jacket, hanging up in a cupboard along a side passage. Verrell tried to remember the two passages from the brief glance he had had of them, and realized that, if the jacket had been at the far end of one of them, the time taken by Trapes to walk the length of the passage, rummage among his pockets for the cigarettes, and walk back to the main corridor would approximate the time Johns would have taken to disconnect the alarm, nip into the exhibition, obtain the painting, and return to the common meeting-place.

If that is what had happened, the next question was: where had Johns hidden the picture? In one of the cupboards? Apparently not. They had been searched. Then how had he disposed of the picture?

Disposed? Was that literally the word? Once he had discovered the vital paper and had abstracted it from the frame there was no longer any reason for retaining either the picture or its frame. The man might have destroyed both — in the gas-stove, for instance?

Satisfied that he had reached a possible solution to the theft of the Bassete, he continued working backwards. Not only was the coup carefully devised and cunningly carried out, but it was obviously the outcome of weeks, or even months, of careful preparation. Possibly since the first attempt on the collection had made such an involved plot necessary — or, more subtly, the first attempt had been deliberately planned in order to scare Sir Edward into doubling the guards.

If so, the plan had succeeded admirably. Once accepted and on the job, the new guard had bided his time until circumstances were propitious; then he had struck. Then, with the same cunning that had marked every step until then, he had stayed on at his job, seemingly as bewildered as anyone else. Probably he was still there.

A quick journey to the Freshman home would settle the matter, by proving him right or wrong. He rose to his feet, and was moving over to the telephone when Roberts entered.

"Could I have your help, sir, with wiring up the points of alarm?"

They finished the work in just over two hours, then gave the whole a thorough testing. Satisfied that nobody was going to find the task of entering his flat without giving notice an easy one, Verrell prepared to leave.

"Any odd street-cleaners around outside?" he asked Roberts.

"I don't think so, sir. I had a careful look."

"Right, I'm off. I should be back fairly early on in the evening, but will check by 'phone."

He drove to the hotel at which Diana was staying.

"How about a drive home?" he suggested.

"Why home? I thought you wanted me to keep away."

"On your own. Not when you have a nice strong man by your side."

"In that case…" She dimpled. "I'm almost ready. With luck father will be away, or I may have some hectic explaining to do. Especially if he brought those silly guests of his down. Why are we going there?"

"I want to show you something that may be of interest."

"Not the painting?"

"Or the ashes." He refused to say anything more, somewhat to her annoyance.

They reached Terrance Hall, and found the owner away, much to his daughter's satisfaction. They went at once to the west wing.

Trapes was on guard.

"You and Johns got over that fuss all right then?" Verrell asked with a casual air.

"Almost, sir," the guard replied with a ghost of a smile. "Leastwise, I have. Don't know much about Johns."

"How's that?"

"He had to leave sudden-like. Had a message the other day from his mother to say she was dying. Two days after that we had a letter from him saying he'd have to stay and look after her affairs. Johns once said as how she had a little money salted away." The guard looked sour.

Verrell nodded thoughtfully. He felt that he scarcely needed further confirmation of his theory. If only he hadn't taken so long to reach it…

Meanwhile, it occurred to him that, twice before, he had visited the collection for the purposes of interrogation, each time when Johns was on duty; and twice, within a matter of hours, he had been attacked. Another link in the chain of reasoning which connected Johns with the theft. No wonder Johns had sent men to beat up and warn off the interfering writer who would persist in asking so many embarrassing questions…

"Where's he gone?"

"London, sir, but I'm not sure whereabouts. He only left a forwarding address."

"Do you know it?"

"Not off-hand, but I might be able to get it."

"Don't bother." There was no sense in chasing something that would undoubtedly prove to be false. "About the thief — was he wearing a coloured or a white shirt?"

Trapes scratched his head. "Can't rightly say, sir. It wasn't as if I saw him clearly, like Johns did."

"You were finding your cigarettes, weren't you?"

"Yes, sir."

"Precisely what did you see of the man?"

"Well, not so much, you might say, sir. I didn't see the bloke's face at all."

"But you told the police "

"I thought at first I had seen it." He scratched his head again. "I've been thinking about it since then. It was Johns who told me what the man looked like."

"Did you even see the man?"

"I must have done that, mustn't I, sir? After all, the picture was stole by somebody, wasn't it?"

"Undoubtedly," Verrell assured the confused man.

"What is all this about?" Diana asked, as they walked on into the collection. "Didn't Trapes see anyone at all?"

"I don't believe so."

"You mean, he lied?"

"Not purposely, but just because Johns made him believe he had seen a man."

"That's not possible."

"Isn't it? I remember one occasion when I went fishing with a dyed-in-the-wool enthusiast. After getting me up at the crack of dawn, although I don't think there was a fish in the entire river, he could scarcely spare time to have breakfast. I got so fed up with the whole business that, for something to do, I kept asking him if he could see the ripples some really big ones were making. At first he didn't see them, but before long he was seeing more than I had."

"What a meany you are!" she protested.

He grinned. "By the time we returned that evening he was telling everyone of the huge fish that kept jumping out of the water, then turned to me for confirmation."

"I still think you're a meany. But where is all this leading to?"

"That there never was a man. Johns said there was, but 130

Trapes merely thought there was one because he heard Johns say so."

"But somebody stole the picture and set off the alarm."

"I'm coming to that. But let's go back to the gas-stove."

"In Heaven's name, whatever for?"

"To look for some ashes. But first…" He inspected the walls with keen eyes.

"What are you looking for?"

"Electric cables."

She sighed. "You're so very lucid, Richard."

He relented, and having tapped his way out of the exhibition rooms into the corridor, tapped his way along the panelled walls until he found what he was looking for.

"Look."

With the help of his penknife he slid the panel away from its frame, and exposed a box-like aperture through which ran a number of separate electric cables. One of these had been cleverly severed to bare a negative wire which had first been cut, and then rejoined with the help of an additional short length of wire.

"See?"

She turned a puzzled face towards him. "No," she confessed. "Tell."

"Johns first cut through the rubber covering, then separated the negative and positive wires so as to avoid fusing them. Then he waited for the right moment. He cut the negative wire, which immediately put the alarm out of commission, went into the exhibition room, took down the Bassete, hid it, and returned here. He then joined the wire up, as you see, which had the effect of setting off the alarm and machinery for sealing off the collection. Simple, isn't it, when you know how?"

"You're a genius," she said with complete sincerity.

He grinned at her. "It's just the way my mind works," he explained.

The drive back to London was, for the most part, a silent affair. This was Verrell's own fault. There was so much to occupy his thoughts.

To begin with, the picture. As he had suspected, he found a small heap of ashes in the gas-oven. Scientific analysis of the ashes would, he was convinced, identify them as those of the late lamented canvas.

Solving the mystery of the theft had helped his *alter ego*, but had not given him the lead he had needed. It had come too late. Johns had left, and his present whereabouts were unknown. What would be his next move? What was Verrell's own move to be?

It was not triumph at his success which produced the quirk on his lips, the twinkle in his eyes. This was brought about by the memory of that pendant, that gossamer-like pendant that had arrested his attention, and prompted his original preliminary exploration of Terrance Hall.

Just when he had given up hope of obtaining it, Fate had played one of her most tantalizing, mischievous pranks. Even as he had stood by the severed alarm cable and pointed out to Diana the way in which the picture had been stolen, the reflection had flashed through his mind that the pendant could be his for the taking, as it were. A flick of the fingers as he pretended to replace the panel — and the alarm would be disconnected for the second time. After that it would be the simplest matter in the world for Blackshirt to return to Terrance Hall and lure the guard from his post just long enough to obtain the pendant.

The thought, quickly created, was as speedily dismissed. He had lost interest in the pendant. For at least three reasons. The first: there was the far more exciting, far more dangerous affair of the stolen Bassetes to hold his craving for adventure. The second: well, one didn't steal from a friend, and although Diana had no personal interest in the pendant, it would have been a knavish trick to take advantage of her friendship and hospitality. The third: — and how important this one was, only he knew — Blackshirt did not follow in the steps of other men. There would have been no fun in using the methods evolved by another; no mental stimulus. As far as Blackshirt was concerned, the pendant would remain in its showcase until the end of time.

Nevertheless, it was amusing…

Before inserting his front-door key into the lock he pressed the knob of a bell which Roberts had cunningly concealed. The valet met him at the top of the stairs.

"Good evening, sir."

" 'Evening, Roberts. Everything in order?"

"Yes and no, sir. I think I have something of interest to show you."

"What is it?" Verrell asked sharply.

"You know the old building opposite, number fifteen, which has recently been converted into flats? I think its occupants are more interested in this flat than you would probably like them to be."

"What makes you think so?"

"The way the drawn curtains keep moving. After I had seen this happen I took the liberty of borrowing your field-glasses."

"Was the result interesting?"

"Very. There's a man behind the curtains who is also using field-glasses."

Verrell chuckled. He did not have to ask why anyone should be using field-glasses in the flat opposite. "Was it like a man bending down to peer through a keyhole and seeing the whites of somebody else's eyes?"

Roberts permitted himself the luxury of a faint smile. "Something of that sort did occur to me, sir," he admitted.

"So things are hotting up, eh, Roberts? I must take a look at our friend opposite."

"You'll find the small room safest, sir. I left the glasses there for you."

"Right."

Verrell had no difficulty in recognizing Sam. He was propped up in a chair, draining the contents of a bottle of beer.

Just before midnight Blackshirt left the flat — long after Sam had given up and retired to bed. He crossed the road.

The house opposite had been divided into three flats, with a common entrance. It took him only a few seconds to force the lock. Once inside the building he switched on his flashlight for a moment, and saw that a common staircase led to the two upper flats. Pausing only long enough to make sure that his entrance had caused no alarm, he ascended the stairs to the second floor. There he pressed his ear against the outer door, and was soon delighted to hear the faint echo of deep snoring.

The door was locked, but the key had been left on the inside. He took a pair of pliers from his belt. These had long, but exceedingly slender jaws which he was able to insert in the lock. With them he secured a grip on the end of the key which enabled him to turn it.

Inside, he found himself in a long passage containing four closed doors. He was interested only in the room sheltering the snoring Sam. There was no difficulty about locating this. He carefully opened the door, and pressed the button of his flashlight. Its narrow beam revealed the sprawling Sam on the bed. With the exception of his jacket, which had apparently fallen off the foot of the bed, he was fully dressed.

Blackshirt collected the jacket and took it into the passage for closer examination. He found nothing of interest in it so he returned to the bedroom and cautiously slipped his hand beneath the pillows. From his knowledge of Sam's type of thug he expected to find something there. He was not disappointed. His sensitive fingers first touched something that felt like a leather wallet, then withdrew it from beneath the pillows with a gentle pull which failed to disturb the sleeping man.

Again he left the bedroom to examine his find. The wallet contained a small bundle of five-pound notes, several newspaper cuttings about greyhounds and their form. Nothing else.

For some minutes Blackshirt was disappointed by the fact that his visit was, for all practical purposes, being wasted. Then, at the last moment, he noticed the telephone which rested on a stool near the head of the bed.

Convinced that the telephone was there for a purpose, he wondered how best to make use of his discovery. A few moments' reflection supplied the answer — but before anything could be done, Sam's sleep, sound as it was, had to be converted into an even sounder unconsciousness.

From his belt he extracted a small phial of chloroform which he always carried with him for use in such emergencies.

He borrowed one of Sam's own filthy handkerchiefs, saturated it with the liquid, and carefully pressed it down upon the other man's bulbous nose.

Then he reached for the telephone.

Chapter Thirteen

It was highly probable that Sam had to report by telephone the results of his surveillance, so that his employer could build up a picture of Verrell's habits, try to find a weak point at which to strike, or hope to get a lead on Diana...

He dialled nought. After the usual long wait he was able to explain what he wanted to a bored operator, who indignantly denied that anyone could possibly handle such a request at that hour of the night. But even over the 'phone Blackshirt had a charm that often enabled him to get by where others would fail. After three minutes' hard talking he was put on to a supervisor.

"Yes?"

"I'm speaking from Hanton two-one-one-six, and I'd like to make an enquiry about some calls that were made from this number earlier in the day."

"Do you realize...?" the supervisor began with a snap.

"Yes, of course, and I do apologize, but you see..." The story was long and involved, but it was so convincing that it went a long way to show why he was a successful author.

"I'll see if anything can be done," the supervisor grudgingly agreed. "I'll ring you back..."

During the wait he checked on Sam. Sam was still completely unconscious, but Blackshirt added a few more drops of the chloroform as good measure. Sam was still in the same condition when the 'phone bell rang.

"Hanton two-one-one-six?"

"Yes."

"'Were you making enquiries about outgoing trunk-calls?"

"Yes."

"There have been three during the past twenty-four hours/"

"Good. I appreciate the trouble you have taken."

The tone of voice became perceptibly warmer. "All three were to the same number, Penfield three-six, and each was of six minutes' duration."

"I suppose you wouldn't know the address of Penfield three-six?"

128

"I can look it up. Hold the line." The man was not long in finding out the required information. "Penfield three-six is at Queen's Hall, Scot field, Hampshire."

"Very many thanks... Blackshirt laid the thanks on with a trowel.

Having replaced the receiver, he took stock of the situation. There was no immediate hurry to visit that address, he concluded. In a sense events were waiting on him. Parson and company wanted the two pieces of paper in his possession, and could do nothing in the matter of the hidden loot until and unless they could wrest them from him. He, in turn, was similarly stymied until he obtained their two. In those circumstances, he could afford to wait until the following night before travelling south. A decision which accorded well with his leaning towards a spot of sleep.

He left the flat as silently as he had entered. Some time later Sam threw off the effects of the anaesthetic, regained consciousness, and wished he hadn't. His head throbbed, and as for the taste in his mouth — to say nothing of the sick feeling...

He almost resolved to stop drinking in future...

Verrell allowed plenty of time for his journey the next day. For one thing, he was travelling in a saloon car, which meant that he was unable to travel as quickly; for another, the day was so perfect that he was content to take things easily.

Back in London, sick, miserable Sam still watched the flat, although Verrell had left it in full view of the watcher. He had done this by sending Roberts out to buy a white apron, 136 peaked cap, and a metal tray with six bottles of milk. Roberts had then 'delivered' the milk, handed the apron, cap and tray to Verrell, who took away 'the empties'.

Scotfield was deep in the Hampshire countryside, ten miles from the London-Portsmouth road. To reach the village one had to travel through roads whose twisted turnings and narrowness would not have disgraced Romney Marsh. The village itself had a green, a church of ancient tradition and much restoration, the customary and essential inn, and the almost as important general stores. Queen's Hall lay away from the green, along a small side road which might have led somewhere — but probably didn't.

He drove slowly past the house. There was not much to see, thanks to the fact that it was surrounded by a brick wall some seven feet high and broken, as far as he could judge, only by a large pair of wrought-iron gates which gave access to a short drive. He continued along the rising road in the hope that he might gain an elevation from which he would be able to see more of the house. Unfortunately, just at a moment when he believed his hope was justified, the road took a sudden turn to the right, then dipped down into a hairpin bend which would have taxed Ascari's skill.

He had dinner at a public-house some distance off. As soon as it was dark he returned to Queen's Hall, parked his car in an inconspicuous side road, made his way across two intervening fields, and reached the rear of the property.

As he had anticipated, the wall he had seen from the road enclosed the house. It was, if anything, higher at the back than at the front — a monument to the times when a 'brickie' was allowed to lay as many bricks as he wished. He followed the wall round, retracing his steps to the road. There was only the one gate, it seemed; and from the sound of heavy throat-clearing and expectoration which came from the inside, it was apparent that a man was stationed there.

As an obstacle, the wall itself did not rate very high, he considered. A jump, and he would be able to catch hold of the top and haul himself up and over. But cursory examinations were never good enough for Blackshirt. He took out his torch checked that the shutter was all but closed, then pressed the button. The tiny spotlight illuminated only where it touched. As he directed it at the top of the wall it produced two quick flashes which told him all he wanted to know — what he had seen earlier was indeed a wire, two in fact, and they ran the length of the wall. Convinced that they were electrified, he realized that they would make any attempt to scale the wall exceedingly unprofitable.

Further examination showed him that the wires stood out from the wall at such an angle that a ladder would be useless. A large one would rest against the wires; a smaller one would leave the climber the task of surmounting them — an impossible feat of balance.

He could cut the wires, of course. But it was pounds to a penny that they also acted as an alarm which the mere act of touching would set off. Characteristically, he wasted no further time in trying to find a way of entry over the wall. There remained only the gates.

To make use of the official entrance to the grounds meant that the man must be removed, and the gates opened. He evolved idea after idea, each one designed to achieve this object, but discarded each in turn as it proved theoretically unworkable. Much of the trouble was due to the fact that the gates fronted the road. Cars were infrequent, but he dared not risk taking their absence for granted. So, for want of inspiration, he studied the gates from the shadow of the hedge opposite. After ten minutes or so he heard a shuffling of feet on the gravel drive, and through the gates saw the glow of a cigarette.

How to get the man to open the gates and welcome Blackshirt with a gesture of brotherly love, or as a long-lost friend? A hopeless proposition, seemingly; and yet, presently, two factors clicked together, and an idea was bom. One that needed more than a spice of luck for success, but still — for want of a better...

When he had driven past the house earlier in the day he had noticed a television aerial — one of those elaborate affairs which seem to stretch in all directions. If the inhabitants of the house should chance to be watching a television programme... He checked on the time, thought it more than likely. If they weren't, then his plan would not ruin any 138

alternative he might think up; if they were, then it could succeed, might well succeed.

First, to obtain a car. Preferably an old one, with magneto ignition. He moved cautiously along the far side of the road, and made for the village green. The public-house was on the near side; just beyond was a patch of land used as a car park. In it were two cars: one all mouth-organ grins and willowy springing, the other so ancient, so dilapidated, he was sure that it must belong either to a man with a sense of humour or to a titled man of immense wealth. He chose the ancient.

There was a slope with a gradient that would allow the car to freewheel half-way round the square. He released the brake, gave the car a push, and had the satisfaction of seeing his estimate of freewheel distance easily exceeded. As soon as the car was well away from the pub he put it into gear. The engine spluttered into life. He drove from the village at high speed.

Inside Queen's Hall there was a complete lack of harmony. Parson was in charge of the other men, but he lacked the ability to command. In consequence there were continual arguments and loud expressions of ill-feeling. Jim was perpetually thirsty, and wanted to spend his evenings in the local. He had been roughly told that he must stay in the house until further notice, and sulked in consequence. Stevenson had only lately joined the gang, but was as loud in complaint as any. He had a streak of viciousness in his make-up that had twice landed him in gaol with lengthy sentences. One way and another, the three men snapped and snarled at each other until their tempers wore dangerously thin.

At first, with the coming of night, their humour had been slightly restored by their having succeeded in obtaining a crate of beer. Added inducement to better spirits was supplied by the T.V. programme: amateur boxing, a subject they could all understand.

"Smash him one," ordered Stevenson, speaking to one of the diminutive figures. "Use your left. Use your ruddy left." He had a ten-shilling wager with Parson on the result.

"Pipe down," snapped Jim. "I want to hear what the commentator has to say."

"Open your lugs then.1'

"Can't you two ever shut up?" Parson snapped.

"Look who's talking," jeered Jim.

For a time the three men were silent as the fighters exchanged a flurry of blows in the centre of the ring. Both the silence and the boxing were interrupted by the bell.

"Listen to that," Stevenson shouted with excitement as a commentator began an inter-round summary. "The last round went to my bloke in blue pants, Fisher."

"Don't be a blasted fool," exclaimed Parson violently, "you put your money on the chap in white shorts, 'Knock-Out' Scott."

"That I didn't "

"Like hell you did."

The heated argument continued, with neither man listening to the other, until Jim took a poor view of the interruption.

"For God's sake shut up so as I can watch the flipping fight," he yelled.

The other two were on the point of obliging when a series of lines spread across the screen and reduced the picture to a meaningless blur.

"Blasted cars!" shouted Stevenson.

The picture remained jumbled, but the voice of the commentator carried on with increasing excitement. 'Knock-Out' Scott, it seemed, was staggering under a very good blow to the chin; it seemed doubtful that he would last out the round.

"That's ten bob you owes me," chortled Stevenson.

"Like hell! It's your man who's nearly out."

The picture remained an incredible jumble of black and white lines.

"Get the hell out of it," Stevenson snarled, as though he was trying to make sure that his voice would reach the motorist outside and goad him on to worry someone else. "Here, Jim, go out and tell the blighter we're trying to look-see. Smash his nose if he gets funny."

"Do it yourself. I'm not moving."

"Go on, Jim, get out there and ask the car to move on." Parson tried to inject some authority into his voice, but failed.

"And your grandmother's hat!"

By now 'Knock-Out' was lying helpless on the canvas, and the count was reaching nine. The bell saved the boxer, but the commentator had no hesitation in prophesying that the fight would finish before the end of the third and last round.

'Til teach the perisher," snarled Stevenson. "You keep an eye on Mister Ruddy Parson, and see he doesn't pinch the money." He jumped up from his seat, and hurried out of the room. The door slammed behind him.

Andrews, at the gate, saw Stevenson emerge from the front door with a rush. "What's up, mate?" he asked pleasantly. "Place on fire, or something?"

"It soon will be if something doesn't happen. The T.V. screen's like a jig-saw puzzle. Car out in the road somewhere, with its engine running."

"I thought I was hearing something."

"You thought — Gawd! A deaf man could hear that ruddy noise. Open those gates so as I can give the bloke a piece of me mind."

"Don't be too rough." Andrews grinned as he unbolted and unlocked the gates.

Stevenson walked to his left, where he could hear but not see the offending car; gradually as his eyes became accustomed to the darkness he was able to distinguish the outline of the car.

"Where are you?" he yelled with a savage voice.

"Here," he heard a voice from behind answer.

He turned as Blackshirt pressed the button of his torch. The strong beam dazzled the irate Stevenson; simultaneously, it illuminated a belligerent chin that positively asked to be punched. It was punched.

Blackshirt picked up the unconscious body, slung it over his shoulders, and walked along the road until he reached a gate that opened into a small paddock. He dropped Stevenson on the far side of the hedge, used his belt to secure his legs, a length of rope to fasten his hands, and his own handkerchief to act as a gag.

Blackshirt returned to the car, switched off the engine.

133

"Hey, come out here, and have a look at this blooming engine," he shouted, in fair imitation of the unconscious Stevenson.

Andrews left the gates and walked along to the car. He peered into the darkness. "Where the hell are you?" he called out in an aggrieved voice.

Stevenson would have liked to answer.

Like a black shadow Blackshirt moved swiftly through the open gates, and advanced towards the house. In front it fairly blazed with light, for several windows were uncurtained, and the front door stood open. So he skirted the front and continued on round to the back. Only one window there showed any light, he was glad to see, and it was on the first floor.

He found a door which opened at his gentle push with the faintest of protests from the hinges. Just in case even this slight sound had been heard, he paused for a while before going further into the house, but the noise from a television set above made it ninety per cent certain that his entrance had passed unnoticed. He moved forward, and found himself in a short passage which ended at a glass door.

Enough light passed through the glass to enable him to dispense with his torch. When he reached the door and looked through he saw the main hall beyond. He also saw, close to the door on the other side, a series of electric-light switches. In the hope that one of them was a two-way switch to control the hall light, he cautiously opened the door and reached for the switches. The second one he tried did the trick, and plunged the hall into darkness. Another short pause, to make certain that nobody had noticed the lights go off, and then he ascended the staircase.

Behind the door nearest to the upper landing, voices were still arguing loudly above the boxing commentary; Parson maintained that he had backed the winner, Jim just as vigorously defended the claim of the absent Stevenson. Blackshirt moved on, and having ascertained that the next room was in darkness, he entered.

A quick examination showed the room was of the type so beloved of the Victorians, and named by them a study. It was complete with desk, the inevitable bookcases, and in one corner a safe, which he decided to investigate if the opportunity offered itself. Meanwhile, there were other rooms to be explored; the one opposite, for instance. He crossed the land-

142

ing, entered it. A bedroom, this, but he paid little attention to the room itself, for, hanging on one wall, was a painting that he was ready to swear was a Van Dyck — which convinced him that he was probably looking at one of the five Bassetes. With swift movements he crossed the room and examined the frame. It was a Bassete sure enough, for he found an aperture in the frame in which an oblong piece of paper could easily have been hidden — but the aperture was empty.

He had no time to do more than re-hang the picture. The 'phone bell rang.

First things first. Blackshirt looked about him for a convenient place of concealment.

The sound of the 'phone bell brought the argument between Parson and Jim to a summary conclusion. Parson left, to answer the call. He was absent for nearly ten minutes. As soon as he returned he went across to the television set and switched the programme off.

"What the hades..." Jim began.

"That was the boss. Where's that blasted Stevenson?"

"How should I know?"

"Go out and find him."

Jim would have argued, but Parson had used the magic words. One did not argue with the boss. Not if one valued one's well-being. He went out to the landing and bawled. When Stevenson failed to appear Jim muttered angrily, stumped down the stairs, and went to have a word with Andrews.

In due course he returned. "He's done a bunk," he told Parson.

Parson was justifiably incredulous. "Don't talk blasted nonsense."

Jim looked aggrieved. "Well, he ain't in the house, he ain't in the grounds, he ain't anywhere in the road, so where is he?"

"If he's gone to the pub I'll break every bone in his damn' body."

"Can't a bloke even have a drink?"

"You've had one case of beer. What more do you want?"

"Another case."

"You won't get it, so shut up. And when Stevenson gets back he'll learn to do what he's told, or else!" Parson ignored his companion's snort of derision. "You and I have to go up to London tomorrow."

"What for?"

"To snatch the Freshman woman, damn her eyes! The boss has found out where she is staying."

"Where?"

"Some hotel in Piccadilly."

"Come off it!" Jim was alarmed. "We're not expected to grab her out of there, are we?"

"Use your common, can't you? She isn't going to stay in the blooming place all day. She'll be out sometimes. That'll be our chance."

"You hope!" exclaimed Jim, who was somewhat of a pessimist. "What about that blasted Verrell?"

"He'll see sense quick enough when he finds out where his girl's got to." Parson's eyes glistened. "I only hope I'm there when he gets the news, the swine."

"You're not the only one what wishes that," Jim agreed with a vicious snap. "Where's he got to, anyway?"

"Boss says Sam's been watching the flat all day, but he hasn't moved out once."

"Why don't we grab him in the flat then, and cut out the girl?"

"Like you did last time, I suppose!"

"You weren't so ruddy clever yourself, when it came to using a gun," Jim sneered.

Parson repressed the mounting tension with an effort. "Carr's coming down tomorrow afternoon. See that Stevenson makes everything ready for the girl."

"If you asks me," Jim sulkily commented, "we'll have earned that five thou, by the time we get it."

Conversation became desultory, finally withered. Parson yawned several times; Jim loudly belched as he finished the last bottle of beer.

"Wish I knew where Stevenson got to," Parson said as he made for the bedroom.

"Rotten little swine."

Parson nodded agreement as the two men disappeared into their respective bedrooms.

An hour later Blackshirt stood before the safe, inspecting its possibilities. It was modern, but not too modern, he decided. Patience and skill would succeed in opening it.

He fixed a stethoscope to his ears, flexed the fingers of his gloved right hand, and began to manipulate the dials. The work was slow and tedious, and had to be performed with every sense tuned up to concert-pitch. Especially hearing, for not only had he to listen to the tiny clicking sound which would inform him that he had achieved the first letter of the combination, but at the same time he had to remain alert for any suspicious noise in the house.

His touch had to be equally delicate — it would be so easy, so damnably easy to move the dials that thousandth part of an inch which would prevent the tumbler from falling — which would mean his having to complete the circle again and again and again. In fact, in time he was forced to admit that he had missed the combination, so he started again.

After an hour his tiring fingers warned him that he must take a rest. He relaxed in one of the easy chairs, and wished he dared light a cigarette. After ten minutes' rest he started again on the wearisome and monotonous task of opening the safe.

Excluding the ten minutes' rest, it took him five minutes short of two hours to discover the combination and open the safe. Only to find it almost like Mother Hubbard's cupboard. Bare. But not absolutely so. The two missing pieces of paper were not there, greatly to his disappointment, but there was a thick wad of Bank of England notes to which he had the very greatest pleasure in helping himself.

There was also an empty envelope — but it had on it an address in the seventeenth arrondissement of Paris, so he took that too, in case it might be useful. Having thus cleared the safe, he closed it, and then made his way downstairs and out into the garden.

He was now faced with the problem of breaking out of the grounds, for greatly to his astonishment he saw that the gates were still guarded — Heaven alone knows why! he reflected — though by a shorter, stockier man than Andrews. At the same time he proposed to try and contrive a method of re-entry, in case the prospective visitor of the following afternoon might have the pieces on his person. In case he had, well, a little ingenuity might effect a transfer — it was worth trying — if he could get back into the house again...

He grinned. If — if — if...! All so simple, if...! Meanwhile, he was hoping to find some sort of transformer and switch box, for it was doubtful that the wires running above the outer wall were connected directly with the mains supply — that would be too dangerous.

He found the transformer. It was housed in an iron box attached to the side of the house, with an exterior switch — a makeshift affair, one way and another, but apparently efficient. A heavy electric cable from the house had been fed into the bottom; two bare wires emerged from the top, ran up the wall for eight feet or so, and then crossed the intervening space to the wall.

It was soon evident what he would have to do. Two lengths of strong twine would have to be attached to the switch, one to pull the switch down and off, the other to pull it up and on, and then threaded through anything that would serve as a rough type of pulley in such a way as to provide a pull-switch of rough-and-ready design.

He returned to the house and searched first through the kitchen, then in a cupboard under the stairs. He found a ball of twine, but it had the disadvantage of being white. A trip back to the study, and the appropriation of a bottle of ink, soon changed its colour.

Trying to create the pulley effect proved a headache, but he finally solved the problem by making use of a window nearby. By boring holes through the woodwork at the corners he was, after some improvisation, able to create the effect he wanted.

He paid out the two lengths of twine to a short distance from the window, and pulled the one designed to switch off the current. Precisely nothing happened.

He tried again, with the same result. A check showed that the twine was catching on the edge of the hole he had bored for it. He fined down the edges of both holes, and tried once more. This time the switch worked. He pulled on the other length, and the switch went on again.

He switched off once more, paid out the twine as far as the wall, then threw the rest over. Then he followed suit by jumping up and catching hold of the edge of the bricks with 146

his hands. A pull, an athletic twist, a heave, and he was up and astride the top.

He dropped down on the far side, and heaved on the twine. He heard the faint echo of a click as the current was switched on again. He tucked the ends of the twine under a clump of dock leaves.

"Now for our friend in the meadow," he told himself as he straightened up. 'Til bet he's mad."

Chapter Fourteen

Stevenson returned to consciousness feeling rightfully aggrieved. His jaw ached. His head ached. Everything ached. He wanted to know just what the hell was going on. Somebody was going to suffer. When he tried to move, he made the disconcerting discovery that it would probably be himself.

His feet and legs were bound neatly and expertly. When he tried to shout, his dazed brain registered for the first time the fact that a large and dirty handkerchief had been forced into his mouth. It tasted foul. His ill-humour would not have improved had he known it was his own.

While he was swearing harshly an amazing thing happened. Without warning, he was suddenly picked up as though he weighed nothing, and carried across two fields. Then he was dropped down, the gag was taken out of his mouth, and a tiny spot of light was played over his face.

"Not a very pleasant specimen," remarked Blackshirt pleasantly.

"Who the?"

"Not so loud. Never know who's around."

Stevenson wanted to cry out and tell the unknown man where to go. Something made him hold his tongue. At the same time he began to feel frightened.

"Good. I see I don't have to warn you not to shout. Now we're here, care to answer a few questions?"

"No, I "

"How long have you been mixed up with all this nonsense?"

"Nonsense!" For a brief space of time he considered the description. "I don't know what you're talking about."

"No?"

"No."

"Were you in on that robbery down in Hampshire? The one where a man got severely beaten up?"

"Here, I "

"You were." Blackshirt correctly diagnosed the strained expression. "How long have you been with this outfit?"

"Nearly a year," he answered sullenly.

"Just the right sort of time to leave. How much have you been paid during this time?"

"Never you mind."

"How much?"

Stevenson thought he ought to answer. From the tone of the man's voice if he didn't he might very soon regret his silence. The absence of a figure to go with the voice was a threat he could not measure. The ease with which he had been picked up and carried along was another.

"Ten pounds a week when nothing's doing."

"And when something is?"

"A hundred."

"How much is your share when it's all over?"

"Five thousand."

"Much too much. Lead you into bad ways," mocked Blackshirt. "Just as well you won't be collecting."

"Who says I won't?"

"When I let you free I doubt if you'll be in much of a hurry to return."

The words acted as a tonic. Up to that moment Stevenson had not reckoned on going free. Instead, his imagination had been working overtime. Hearing the welcome news, he became pugnacious.

"You'd better set me free, mate. And be quick about it. If you don't, I'll make you wish you'd never ruddy well set eyes on me."

Blackshirt laughed. "Excellent. But how will you know me if you do see me again?"

There was a deep silence. For all he knew, Stevenson was addressing an Outer Mongolian.

"You see my point?"

There was no answer.

"Luckily, I have a kind heart. I'll explain a few things. You know the safe in the study?"

"What study?"

"In the house you so lately left."

"What if I do?"

"There used to be a lot of money in it. Over a thousand pounds. Ever think of trying to open it?"

"I ain't no perishing screwsman."

"I thought that was rather outside your line of country. There's not much of an artistic soul about you. To get back to the money. It's no longer there."

"What d'you mean?"

"I've just taken it."

A pause was followed by a curse. Stevenson had finally decided it was impossible for him to escape from the bonds. "So you're clever!" he finally sneered.

"No," denied the other modestly. "But while I was about it I had a good idea. I put your cigarette-case inside the safe before I relocked the door."

Another pause. Which lasted until the full meaning of this act became apparent. "Here, I ain't... You haven't..." "If you don't believe me, have a look for the case when I let you go."

The suggestion was perfectly safe. Blackshirt had taken the case from the other's pocket on the journey across the fields.

"You can see the result? Your Commander-in-Chief approaches the safe to withdraw a fiver to buy a packet of cigarettes. He opens the door, can hardly believe his eyes. He becomes annoyed. Because he wanted a cigarette," he explained lightly. "Becoming annoyed he wants to know who was the clever person. If he's very bright he will notice your cigarette-case. The connection will be rather obvious."

It was. "You dirty "

"Let's skip the details."

Stevenson remained silent. He knew Carr. He could imagine what Carr would have to say in the circumstances which had just been outlined. Before he, Stevenson, knew what was happening he'd be looking at the sky through six feet of earth.

"Frankly, if I were you, I'd move elsewhere," Blackshirt suggested.

"How can I? I can't move a ruddy inch."

"We can remedy that. I'll take these bonds off and leave you to carry on. Being kind-hearted, here's a couple of notes to see you through the next few days."

The moment he was free Stevenson made a desperate attempt to fight the man who had cornered him so successfully. It was useless. Returning circulation doubled him up with pain.

After what seemed hours the agony ceased. He prepared to meet the voice which had been mocking him for so long. But he was alone. He began walking. He felt very sad and sorry for himself.

Verrell 'phoned Diana before breakfast. This clearly shewed the urgency of the matter.

"Richard, what on earth's wrong? I'm still asleep! Don't say you've already been for a long walk and written a couple of chapters, or I'll throw something."

"Don't be so uncomplimentary."

"You forget I know you slightly."

It was five minutes before he came round to the reason for his early call.

"Don't move from your hotel until you hear from me."

"But why this sudden warning? That's what you said last time and I've been such a good little girl. Gone to bed early — haven't stayed out late once!"

"I'm talking about the daytime as well. Don't move out of the hotel, whether it's two in the afternoon or morning."

"Don't be ridiculous, Richard! I've an appointment with my hairdresser today."

"Cancel it."

"What?" Her voice was incredulous.

"You heard."

"You're a beast, Richard! All very well for you to treat the matter lightly, but if you could see the state my hair's in you'd show some sympathy!"

He laughed. "It's probably just as perfect as it always is." "Stop talking nonsense. Aren't you ever going to take me out to lunch again?"

"Not today. Too much work to do."

"You're very unchivalrous and I can't think why I put up with it."

"On the contrary, you'd be surprised by the dragons I'm going forth to slay."

"For heaven's sake, don't go and get yourself burnt up."

"I won't."

The conversation closed soon afterwards. Roberts brought in the breakfast.

"How's our friend across the way? Still on the job?" "Yes, sir. I checked just now and he had the glasses trained on us. Some more coffee, sir?"

"Another cup might restore my faith in human nature! I'm going out later on. You'd better deliver the milk again." "Very good, sir. When will you be leaving?"

Verrell thought for a moment. He had to visit Otto Speyer, source of so much information… among other things.

"An early lunch, I think, and I can go immediately afterwards."

He spent the morning working. Rather necessary since his publishers were expecting the completed manuscript within a matter of weeks.

Otto Speyer was a big fence. His income would have made any self-respecting tax inspector — had any one of them known about it — lick his lips with joy. So big had he become, he could not be bothered to deal with stolen jewellery unless it was relatively valuable. When he could be bothered, one either sold to Otto, or else…!

He was ruthless. Feared by most. While he feared only one man. Blackshirt. It was partly psychological; partly that not knowing the identity of the impudent cracksman he could not shop him. Thus he was obliged to pay Blackshirt prices that actually approximated half value.

To show he was an honest citizen, Speyer ran a pawnshop. He was sitting behind the counter, when he heard the thump of footsteps from overhead.

Revolver in hand, he crept upstairs. He approached a door, was about to fling it open when he was forestalled. Blackshirt stood there, grinning behind his hood.

"I thought you'd never get here, Otto."

"How did you know…?"

"How? You sounded like a herd of hippopotami coming up the stairs. Come along in, I want a little chat."

The other's lips twitched. He felt nervous, could do nothing about it. "My customers downstairs…"

"Let them be. If they pinch anything you'll be able to buy it back!"

"What do you want? It's most unusual for you to come in the daytime."

"Never mind, you'll get used to the routine being upset. For heaven's sake, sit down, Otto. You're acting like a jelly. I've only come for a little assistance."

"What kind?"

"I want something — and you were the only person I could think of at short notice to help me."

"You want something… these days you always want something. In the old days you used to bring me jewellery to buy." Otto spoke with feeling. Despite the fact that Blackshirt was as hard a bargainer as himself, there had always been a very handsome profit at the end of a sale. Mainly because the cracksman had always chosen such superb examples of the jeweller's art.

"We must do something about this. What would you like?"

"The Mentmore rubies." He spoke without hesitation. There was a man who would pay as much for the stones as they would fetch in the open market.

"Right. As soon as I've a spare moment, I'll bring them along."

Speyer mumbled "Yes." Inwardly cursed. He never knew whether his visitor was serious.

"Now, back to the immediate. I want one of those guns they issue to bank clerks and mail guards. The type which fires a dye."

"I have heard of such things/" said the other cautiously.

"Further, it must be the new type. Looks like an ordinary revolver and holds six cartridges."

Speyer blew his nose. "How can I get hold of such a thing?" He shrugged his shoulders. "People do not pawn that kind of gun."

"Nevertheless, I want one."

"I say again — I do not know how I would get such a weapon." There was still no reaction. "And it would be very expensive."

"So's salt in the Congo," retorted Blackshirt good-humouredly. "Rustle round and get hold of one pronto."

"I'll try. But it will be difficult. Even if I find one it may cost as much as "

"Five pounds?"

Speyer grimaced. "You will joke. Fifty pounds may not be enough by half."

"Five pounds."

He cursed himself. He cursed Blackshirt. Then he 'phoned a person who knew a person. Between them, those two could supply anything from a forged passport to an outsize steel girder. Between them they had what was wanted. It would cost sixty pounds.

Three minutes later the sum had dropped to five pounds; the air was tinged with blue; accusations and threats had been freely bandied about.

"It will be brought here," said Speyer. "He did not like having to part with it at such a price," he added sadly.

Blackshirt reached the wall surrounding Queen's Hall and paused. His arrangement of twine to switch oh the electricity had been as invisible as he could manage. But it would not pass unnoticed if a close inspection of the grounds had been made. He moved at a snail's pace, reaching forward with each foot in turn to clear obstacles; never transferring his weight until certain it was safe to do so. All the time his ears were strained to catch the slightest sound of muffled breathing or movement. He heard nothing.

He reached the twine, stood still for a long five minutes.

Satisfied that his presence the night before had gone undetected, he pulled the twine. Faintly came the click of the switch. As a final test he caught hold of the top of the wall with one hand and held an insulated pair of pliers against the lowest wire with the other. Nothing happened. A quick pull upwards and he wriggled his way over the top of the wall, forcing apart the two lower wires to get through.

The house was dark except for a light in the hall. He entered by the back door, ascended to the first floor, and after quick deliberation chose to wait in the bedroom. He was only just inside when there was the noise of an approaching car. Through the windows, which fronted the road, he saw it stop. A man jumped out, walked to the gate, had a quick word with the guard.

The gates were opened, the car drove in. As soon as it stopped by the front door two men got out. One was a new face. The other Blackshirt had last seen at the Freshman house.

Carr... alias Johns... stamped into the hall.

"First damned thing is a drink."

"You can say that again," muttered his companion. "It's getting quite chilly at night. Think the rest of the bunch will've left any liquor?"

"I've got some whisky upstairs. Keep it locked."

They mounted the stairs, entered the study. Carr crossed to the small desk, opened one of the small drawers with a key. He put a bottle on the top.

"Glasses are behind you."

They took the spirit neat, in well-ordered gulps.

"Got any cigarettes, Seeton? T've run out."

The other handed his case over. "Things have slowed down, haven't they? We were supposed to have everything buttoned up by today."

Carr shrugged his shoulders angrily. He poured himself out another drink. "First Schmidt played the ruddy fool; then Verrell. It's always the same if one's not there personally to see the job done."

"Who the hell is this Verrell?"

"Writer. Stayed with the Freshmans when I was there."

"He the chap the boys went along to give the once-over?"

"Yes."

"And that's where Sam got his arm busted?"

"It is." Carr's mouth tightened. "If the fool still hadn't some use, it would have been his last job."

"What I can't understand is why you don't pull this fellow in. He's got the paper you want, the one he got from Schmidt."

"That's not the only one. He's had the luck of the devil. But the run's over. I've got the boys watching both him and the Freshman girl."

"I could use another." Seeton indicated his empty glass.

"Pour it. Leave me out. While you're doing that I'll get the money out." Carr crossed to the safe. "The boys'll want their pay — though I'm damned if any of them are worth it. As for that swine Stevenson..." He was opening the door.

"What made him move so suddenly?"

"How should I know? All because a car... Here, what the...? The damned safe's been emptied." He was shouting.

"Emptied. Can't be."

"Look for yourself. Some bright boy's pinched everything. Who the?"

"It was I," said Blackshirt correctly, as he entered the room. He carefully closed the door behind him, pointed the gun impartially at the two men.

Seeton's right hand darted towards his pocket. He froze as the muzzle of the gun settled firmly in the direct line of his stomach.

"That's better. I do hate having to use violence!"

"God!... It's Blackshirt." Carr recognized the figure.

The newcomer bowed mockingly. "Now if you'll be good enough to move away from the safe."

"Blackshirt!" Seeton showed his astonishment — and awe.

"I said, move away from that safe."

Carr did so. He had a gun in his pocket. He knew how to use it. But for the moment he did not consider trying.

"Cross your hands at the back of your necks. A trifle uncomfortable, but I shan't keep you long enough to make it really painful."

The two looked at each other. Then again did as ordered.

"What do you want, Blackshirt?" asked Carr.

"I'm not very particular at the moment. What can you offer?"

"Nothing in your line of country. Certainly nothing to warrant a visit from you."

Carr's brain was working at speed. He tried to assess the possibility of help, remembered how his forces were dispersed. He decided there was no hope in that direction.

"One never knows!"

Carr was thinking about Stevenson. He had disappeared the day before. Now Blackshirt had broken through the defences of the house which up to then he, Carr, had thought impregnable. It was the kind of coincidence he did not like.

"How did you get in?"

"Over the wall."

"Impossible. It's electrified."

"So that's what tickled."

For a moment Carr appeared impressed — but he quickly recovered.

"It was Stevenson."

"And who might he be — another of your beauties?" "When I get my hands on him he'll spend the rest of his short life wishing he'd thought of something else to do with his spare time."

"No ill-feeling, please. And Seeton, don't move your hands away from your neck."

Seeton stiffened.

"I must be off," he continued. "First, a quick look through your pockets. In case you have a gun or two hidden away. I have a constitutional dislike to being potted in the back."

He moved forward until the gun was pressed into Carr's stomach. With expert hands he removed first the gun, then the wallet from the inside pocket.

"What the hell? Put that wallet back."

"Temper, temper." He pressed the gun a little deeper. "Look, Blackshirt, there're some private papers that can't possibly interest you, but they're as important as hell to me." It was hard work, trying to speak quietly when he was choking with anger.

"I'll post them back to you." The urgency in the other's voice was all that was necessary to confirm that the vital squares of paper were in the wallet.

"I'll break "

"A blood-vessel if you're not careful/' said Blackshirt blandly. He stepped back two paces, then a third.

Carr was desperate. If the wallet went, months of hard work went with it. Probably any chance of ever reaching von Steiner's loot.

Blackshirt saw Carr's eyes narrow, his frame tense. He waited, then at the last moment side-stepped. Carr crashed to the ground.

Seeton stayed where he was. He was made of lesser stuff.

Blackshirt waited until Carr had scrambled to his feet.

"That was very naughty of you," he observed. He pulled the trigger. The next second the other man's face was covered in a brilliant blue dye.

"You'll benefit as well." He pulled the trigger again and it was Seeton's turn to go blue in the face.

The dye stung their eyes, half-blinded them. Only dimly could they see the black figure.

"Don't spend too much time in the open," suggested Blackshirt. "You might be pulled in on suspicion of one of these mail robberies otherwise." He smashed the electric-light bulb, left the room.

Andrews was enjoying a cigarette when the voice of Carr broke the silence.

"What's that at your feet? Pick it up."

He could see nothing of interest, but did as he was bid. A boot was scientifically applied to the rounded and well-filled seat of his trousers. He was catapulted head first into a large patch of stinging-nettles. The pain was immediate. He was heedless of the fact that the gates opened and closed. Frantically he dragged himself up and scrambled round looking for dock leaves.

Blackshirt stopped just before the outskirts of London to check on the contents of the wallet. It was filled with banknotes. More important were the two squares of paper tucked away. He sang most abominably an aria from *Tosca*.

There remained the problem of the men waiting for Diana. Not forgotting Sam. A threat and a handful of notes would be sufficient to change his allegiance. As for the others…

He tried to coax a few more miles per hour out of the car, failed, settled back wondering why the makes of 'family' English cars were always twenty years behind the times.

Once more he sat down at his desk to examine the strange, incomprehensible rolls of tissue which seemed to be causing so much excitement in the world. In spite of previous disappointments he was excited. Surely, with four out of a probable five rolls now in his possession, he ought to find out something that would suggest, if not the solution, at least a clue of some sort which would offer a lead.

He smoothed out the first sheet...

"Oh no!" he exclaimed.

The same old story. The same number on the same oblong piece of the same paper, with the same corners missing. Yes, the same this time without any doubt, for this piece had the lower comers missing.

"A million to one the other piece has the upper comers missing," he dismally wagered.

He won his wager.

Somebody was crazy. He was not at all sure it wasn't himself! There was only one consolation. If he was crazy then so was Carr, and so was the Schmidt woman — and she wasn't at all the crazy type. If she wanted these pieces of paper so much that she was willing to commit murder for them, then there was good reason for studying them anew.

The hours passed...

Sam had spent another profitless day watching the flat opposite. He was completely bored. A further large quantity of beer had helped him to pass the time away. A fact which explained why, by nightfall, he was keeping watch with his eyes shut. It was, therefore, with a feeling of annoyance that he felt himself being heavily shaken.

"Shove off," he groaned.

"Wake up."

The voice was one he knew. Dimly he realized he had every reason to remember it. He opened his eyes.

Standing over him was Verrell, dressed in evening clothes, white scarf round his neck.

"I want a word with you."

Sam felt the world was being unkind. He groaned.

"I'm getting fed up with your peering into my house all day. Destroys my sense of privacy."

"I ain't been doing anything of the sort," he answered automatically.

"No?... These your binoculars?"

He looked down at the small table by his side.

"Ignoring the possibility of bird-watching, we're only left with my flat. And I don't like it." There was a snap now to Verrell's voice which made the other man wince.

"I ,,

"So you're going to leave in a hurry, or I'll take you apart, limb by limb, to see what makes you tick."

<<j ii

"Exactly. You'll agree to go."

At last Sam found his voice. "You can't…" he began.

"I can. It means you'll be out of a job. But, take my advice and don't worry on that score. It's just possible you would never have collected your five thousand."

"How do you know?"

"And to make certain you don't starve, take these."

The bundle of crisp five-pound notes held Sam's attention with solid force.

"There's five hundred here. More than you're worth; but I have a fatal streak of generosity in my make-up."

Verrell put the money in Sam's hands. The latter acted with a speed seldom associated with him. The money vanished.

"We'll go for a short walk. When I leave you just carry on. In some ways I like you and I don't want to do anything drastic."

Sam was gently propelled towards the door. Still bemused he found himself walking downstairs, out into the road, forward at a pace too quick for his liking. They continued for ten minutes.

"Don't spend all the money on beer. Don't run into Carr again. He might recognize the notes."

Then Sam was alone. For the first time he could think. He thought of Carr and what he would say. Thought of Verrell. Considered the five hundred pounds. Continued on his way.

Chapter Fifteen

There remained the men waiting for Diana. The hour was late and they might have given up. But it was worth a try. He returned to his flat, identified himself as he opened the front door. He went to his safe and sorted out some jewellery. Lord Radnor — and the police — were still wondering how it could have disappeared. He chose a necklace, too heavy to be attractive, and slipped it into his pocket.

The Beauchamp Hotel was in a quiet street at the back of once-fashionable Mayfair. At the end of the street a car was parked, two bored and sleepy men inside. Had it not been for orders too explicit to be ignored, they would both have been in bed some time before.

Verrell watched them and smiled, turned, walked briskly round the square. He found what he was looking for — the back entrance to the hotel. In direct contrast to the magnificent facade, the back door was only an opening with roll-down shutters.

He lifted up a shutter and entered. Three people saw him pass. Only one spoke. He was assistant to the assistant chef.

"What do you want... sir?" he added.

"Are you in charge here?" asked Verrell cheerfully.

"Yes, sir."

"Have you been inspected by the Board of Sanitation and Pig-keeping?"

"The... why, no, sir, we "

"I thought not." And he passed on through.

The assistant to the assistant chef frantically reached for the nearest bottle of brandy. Pig-keeping at the Beauchamp!

The receptionist on night-duty was a beautiful young lady. She spoilt the effect by realizing it.

"May I help you?" she asked. She realized he was handsome.

"I'd like to speak to Miss Freshman, please, on the 'phone."

"It's very late. Would she be expecting you?"

"I want her to come and have a look at the moonlight," he explained.

The girl was troubled. 'There is no moon/1

"Precisely. That's why I want her to come out and see it. Makes it all so uncommon."

Nervously she asked for his name and made the necessary connection. She waved him into a nearby box.

"Richard! Have you got a spark of decency in you? I was in the middle of a glorious sleep," complained Diana.

"You're coming for a walk."

"Don't be ridiculous. Richard, have you had too much to drink?"

"Of all the nasty suggestions."

"You aren't serious?"

"Most certainly I am."

"I give up!"

"Never mind what you do. Hurry up and rise. We haven't got all day."

"No we haven't," she retorted, "but we seem to have all night."

He laughed.

"Will you tell me what it's all about."

"Nothing much. You're going to be kidnapped."

Diana slammed her receiver down on its cradle. She dressed. She wished she didn't like Verrell so much. Then she might get some sleep. She went downstairs.

"Sorry to trouble you," said Verrell. "Must clear one or two things up. Have a cigarette while I brief you."

They lit up. The receptionist watched them with eager awe.

"Down the road a car is waiting. Go out of the hotel, cross the road, walk slowly towards it. When you get alongside, one, or possibly two, people will bundle you inside."

"Ye gods!" she said with feeling.

"Not worried, are you?"

"Heavens, no. Do this sort of thing every day and twice on Sundays."

He grinned. "Good. Then get cracking. Don't worry."

"Worry? I'm enjoying every moment."

Diana walked out of the front door of the hotel. She saw the car, walked towards it.

Jim noticed her first. "Nice bit of skirt," he said with appreciation.

Parson followed his gaze. "You ruddy fool, it's the Freshman girl. Get that door open at the back. You know what you've got to do."

Nerves taut, they watched her approach. When she was two yards away Jim got out of the front and casually opened the back door. As she drew alongside he moved with speed. One arm went round her waist, one over her mouth. A quick twist, and she was inside. He followed her in, slammed the door.

Parson let in the clutch. A voice from the back of the car cut in.

"Going somewhere?" it asked smoothly and dangerously.

Verrell sat back. It was a nice expensive car. It had quiet doors, and nothing had disturbed the attention of the other two men.

"What...?"

"Get out this way, Diana, and have a good sleep. I shan't be troubling you again."

"It's Verrell," muttered Jim in despair.

Parson digested the news. His stomach twitched. "Do something," he suggested.

"With a gun pointing at me head?"

"It is a bit of a stumbling-block," admitted Verrell. He moved his legs to allow Diana to squeeze past.

"Have a good time," she said, as she reached the road.

"I will. Tell the receptionist the moonlight really is magnificent." He waved, shut the door.

Parson moved uneasily.

"Don't get too restless."

»

"Quite. In the meantime, start driving along this road."

"What are you going to do?" asked Parson, nervously.

"What would you suggest? Something quick because I haven't much time. While you're thinking, get cracking. I'll tell you when to turn."

Parson felt distinctly sick. He wished the hell he had managed to shoot the smiling devil when he'd had the chance. To his dying day he'd never know how he missed. It was the wrong adjective to use — as he realized immediately.

"Turn left."

Verrell scanned the street they had entered. He wanted a police-constable. Consequently there wasn't one in sight. Then he had an idea. It wouldn't do to let his friends in the police-station opposite the Gallery get bored with life. He ordered the car to turn left.

Opposite the station he gave an order which made Parson hesitate. Until something cold touched the middle of the back of his neck.

The car turned off the road and mounted the pavement slowly. It headed straight for the door. Verrell jumped out just before the collision.

Parson worked on the principle that it was every man for himself. He jerked frantically at the door to open it and run. It was jammed against the side of the building. He yelled for Jim's help. Unfortunately the other, acting on the same principle, was already twenty feet away.

The police arrived, led by the redoubtable sergeant. These days he did not take his boots off at night. He saw Jim running and gave chase. A constable supported him. Two other policemen took charge of Parson, who had at last managed to get half out of the car.

Jim quickly joined Parson. The sergeant took them inside and accused them of being drunk. Soon had to retract his obvious mistake. He asked to see the driving licence and log-book.

The simple question produced consternation.

Jim had stolen the car some six hours previously.

"I haven't got them with me," carefully explained Parson. "But of course I've got them at home." He tried to smile.

The sergeant looked at him. "You're sure of that?"

"Of course."

There was an interruption. A constable came into the room. "Sarge, look at this! In the back of the car." He held up a necklace.

The sergeant inspected it. He looked first at Parson, then at Jim. "Whose is this?" he asked pleasantly.

He thought he recognized it as part of the collection which had been stolen some time previously. The description was on a board in the same room. He thought he recognized Jim, too.

"Here, that ain't nothing to do with us." Jim, like many of his friends, jumped to conclusions, talked too much, when meeting the police.

"No?"

"No it ain't. And you blokes can't say it is."

"Found in your car?"

"It ain't our ruddy car. I don't know whose car it is, but he's the..."

Too late he stopped.

The sergeant smiled. He ordered some tea.

"Now," he said, "let's get this straight. The log-book and licence are..."

Verrell ate his breakfast abstractedly the next morning. Two more rolls of paper, and... he shrugged his shoulders. And nothing! They took him no further. They were the same size as the others, had the figure fifty-two on them. They also had comers missing. Different comers. So what?

He returned to his reasoning the first time he had seen one of the squares of paper. It still held good. Either all five were necessary to reach the solution — or each one contained it — or only one... In the last case it must be the fifth square, since he had four.

What did the missing corners mean? What did the figures mean? He rose from the breakfast-table as Wright arrived at the flat.

"There should be a law forbidding people to eat at such disgusting hours,*' said the newcomer abruptly.

"Have a heart. It's only just gone ten."

Wright snorted, said nothing, but went into the kitchen. He came back with a cup of coffee. "Damned good fellow, Roberts."

"That's probably the last cup, which he was saving for himself."

"He can make another."

"Before you start complaining, the cigarettes are just behind you."

"Thought for a minute you'd hidden them." He helped himself. "See you've been doing a lot of wiring in the flat. Here and down the hall."

"Light's been very bad lately."

"What makes you think you've changed that? Only thing any of these wires will do is to ring a bell. Expecting visitors?" 164

Verrell answered slowly. He wished Wright were a little less observant. "In a way/'

"What way?"

Verrell grinned.

Wright switched the conversation. "Thinking of going abroad?"

"Why?"

"I thought you might have that idea. In which case a little word of advice."

"Which is?"

"Don't."

"You're being much too enigmatic for me today. Try a sentence of more than one word."

The other drained his cup before answering. "Not so long ago there was a robbery at Sir Edward Freshman's house. A painting was stolen, so ingeniously that the papers christened it the Impossible Crime. It was impossible — except to one man. Blackshirt."

"For the last time, I "

"Never mind. I've told you what I think of you. Next time you want a small favour, see what the answer will be." "Look, I can tell you how "

Wright stubbed his cigarette out, broke into what the other was saying without the slightest hesitation. "That painting was a Bassete. So was one stolen from Hampshire. And from an Art Gallery. Lastly, there's Schmidt... Jackson. He died, returned to life, died again. He had one. I expect that's why he died. Am I right?"

"I wouldn't know."

"I hadn't connected all this up until the day you met Paula in the park and handed her a parcel. That was presumably the genuine Van Dyck. The one stolen the second time the Gallery was broken into. Took the place of the Bassete you were supposed to be giving her."

Verrell thought people like Wright should be repressed. The way the other took a few facts, and from them reached the right answer, was dangerous. To put it mildly.

"Those Bassetes came from France," continued Wright. "Schmidt was in charge of a concentration camp in France. Von Steiner was in France. The two knew each other, were close friends right up to the time the general got killed. But, not quite close enough for Schmidt to know the full truth! You've heard of von Steiner?"

"Vaguely."

"He amassed a very considerable collection of art treasures and so on from plundered homes. This collection has never been traced. Hence my advice."

"And?"

"I've said my fill. Work the rest out for yourself." Wright left, without saying more than a gloomy good-bye.

Verrell regarded the opposite wall. There was still the one painting to go. He believed it was in France at the address he had taken out of Carr's safe. A quick 'phone call would check. It did. The name Veroux — also on the paper with the address — was that of one of the foremost art critics.

He acted immediately. "Roberts."

"Yes sir"

"I'm off to France."

And thirty-five minutes later he was.

He arrived in his Healey at Dover to find a car-ferry leaving in forty minutes, but his request for a passage was laughed at.

"Not at this time of the year, sir. Every boat running full up. There isn't a vacant berth for weeks."

"Any chance of a cancellation?"

"No, sir. Only one more to come, and that's it over there, from the looks of it. Of course, can't say what might happen with a later boat."

Verrell thanked him and moved away. He wanted to get to Paris in double-quick time. The boats were full — probably the airways would be the same. It looked as though he were stuck, so far as taking his car over, unless one of the other cars broke down on the wharf. At that point he had an idea.

He returned from the nearest grocer's shop with a pound of potatoes. He took one out of the bag, strolled across and casually stuck it into the exhaust-pipe of the car which had been a late arrival, and which was about to move into the Customs shed.

The driver pressed the starter. The engine fired, petered 166

out. He tried again. An A.A. man was called. A frantic searching under the bonnet began. The starter ground away. A small knot of harassed officials collected round the stricken car. They began checking their watches. One of them came across to Verrell.

4'Looks as though you might be lucky after all, sir. Not much time to go now. He can't get his car started for love nor money."

"What lousy luck." Verrell spoke without a blush.

The minutes ticked by, and at last defeat was accepted. The driver talked about buying a new car; the wife mentioned a new husband. Verrell was waved past them, taken through the examination shed at speed, and allowed on the ship. In a very short space of time they were away.

He drove to Paris with fiendish brilliance using his horn as freely as the natives — to their surprised annoyance. On the straight he gave the engine everything it had; on comers he went up to the break-away speed. Over the *pav6* he gritted his teeth and hoped.

Only twice was he passed. Once by a sports Delage that just pipped him, the driver of which could be seen shrieking Gallic encouragement to his steed. Once by a vast eight-litre Bentley which swept by at phenomenal speed and sounded like a roll of artillery-fire.

By the time he had reached the centre of Paris he was hot, tired, and thirsty. A condition soon remedied. Denying himself nothing he booked in at a hotel where a thousand-franc note was useful for a cloakroom tip, and enjoyed the luxury of a cold shower. He then left in his car, braved the thousands of would-be suicides circumnavigating the Arc de Triomphe, and reached a small but select restaurant where prices were beyond belief but were matched by the food.

Later, much later, he moved. His objective the Rue Dupont. It lay just off the Place Pereire. A short, slightly curving street, filled with flats. He drove slowly down it noting the numbers. Opposite forty-four he checked his bearings.

He turned at the end of the road to the right, then right again, and came back to the Arc de Triomphe. Two drivers cursed the English car as they unavailingly tried to force their way across its bows.

He reached his hotel, left again two hours later.

Rue Dupont was empty, with scarcely a light showing. He reached the outside door of number forty-four, opened it and entered. A quick glance assured him that the concierge was not awake and filled with the curiosity of her tribe. He passed down a short passageway, then, half-way along it, turned off through the glass-fronted door leading to the floors above. He climbed up the stairs to the third floor, reached the flat.

The lock on the front door was French in design and conception and resisted all efforts to force it with a skeleton-key. In fact, none of them would pass through the keyhole, let alone turn the tumblers. He sighed.

He selected a tiny, but efficient, drill and fitted a bit; drilled several holes grouped so that at last he had one large hole. It was large enough to let him push a keyhole-saw through. With infinite patience he sawed round the lock. The task was made even more difficult by the necessity for absolute silence, but at last he completed the circle but for a very thin strip of wood. He fitted a suction pad, knocked out the circle, drew the tongue of the lock back. The door opened and he stepped inside.

Blackshirt moved to one side and waited. The minutes passed; the silence continued. Satisfied, he switched on his torch. He was in a tiny hall. To his left stretched a long passageway, with several doors along it. Opposite him was what appeared to be a small study, to his right were two sets of double doors. He opened the nearer ones and entered. It was the dining-room.

Along the walls hung several pictures, but not the one he was after. He moved across and through a pair of highly decorated doors into the lounge. A quick flash of his torch revealed the Bassete hanging on the right of the fireplace. He walked towards it and moved the torch until he could make out what was next to it. It was another Bassete. Or, as he wryly thought, a genuine Van Dyck.

If time had not been so precious he might have enjoyed the problem as to which was which. From an artistic standard he could only have tossed a coin. There was, however, one decisive test. Though hardly in the province of any art critic.

He took the painting on the right-hand side down from the wall, after a careful check that it was not wired to an alarm, and searched the frame at the back. He could find nothing. He tried the other painting and was quickly rewarded. The last and final roll of paper was his.

His success was hardly overwhelming. As he placed it in his pocket a muffled sound outside the room made him snap the torch off. As he did so the room was flooded with light at the click of a switch.

He turned slowly. Looked into the muzzle of an automatic pistol.

Behind the gun was a small and dumpy man, with a pointed beard more grey than black. Though he must have been well past sixty, yet he gave the immediate impression of immense vitality.

"Good morning," he said in English.

"Good morning/' Blackshirt half bowed.

"You came after all! This becomes more and more interesting."

"After all?"

"I had a 'phone call this afternoon. I should say yesterday afternoon — no?" Veroux stroked his beard with his free hand. His other hand kept the pistol sharply on its target. "I thought maybe it was all a joke; until I realized one does not call from London to Paris to be funny."

"Who was the call from?"

Blackshirt had summed up the situation and had rightly decided that the Entente Cordiale would not suffer from any action of his.

"I do not know." The other shrugged his shoulders. "I asked, but the answer was — a friend. Did I have a painting by Bassete? Then I should be careful because an attempt to steal it would be made. I laughed. Who would want to steal it — when I have also genuine Old Masters? But I listened, of course."

"I should have liked to know whom I have to thank."

"Maybe you will learn." Veroux looked puzzled. "Some-

thing about your dress makes me think. Black all over. I think... I have it! I visit England a lot. Your papers are often busy describing the famous Blackshirt. You are he?"

"I am."

Veroux smiled broadly. "Now I realize how important is my capture. This is of great interest. It will amuse the Sfiret6 to whom I shall hand you over. They will enjoy success where your Scotland Yard has failed for so many years!"

Without difficulty, Blackshirt correctly came to the conclusion the other enjoyed listening to himself. Excellent. Time was precious.

"You were very clever. I didn't hear a thing until you were at the door," he said.

Veroux chortled. "Once upon a time I stayed with some friends. They were married, but did not get on well together. I learned to tread quietly." His look was completely French.

Blackshirt did what was expected of him. He sniggered.

"So you come to steal my painting! My Bassete! What abominable taste. I only have it because de Marcel claimed it was a Van Dyck. He — the most incompetent art critic the world has ever seen — dared to disbelieve me, Veroux. We had a wager of a million francs. I won. Naturally."

"A million francs under false pretences," Blackshirt murmured politely.

Chapter Sixteen

Veroux made a queer sound. He thrust his chin forward aggressively. "WTiat?" he barked.

"If you took the money, it's high time you returned it. Assuming, of course, there's some honesty in you."

"*Merde!*" The other shouted. He controlled himself. "Explain yourself. If I were younger I'd horsewhip you."

"I don't doubt it," remarked Blackshirt.

"A man steals into my flat and calls me dishonest. I shall not forget. The Surete know how to deal with such insolence. A Veroux called dishonest!"

"I didn't say it was intentional," he explained. "Merely, that you lost the bet."

"You are a fool. How when I said the painting was by Bassete, was I wrong? Even de Marcel had to agree. That incompetent."

"On the contrary. He was quite correct. It was, and is, a Van Dyck.'

"*Salaud!*" muttered the infuriated man.

"When did you get this other painting?" he asked, ignoring the outburst.

"Lately, maybe five years," mumbled Veroux, between a further flood of bitter words.

"I mean the one you say is by Van Dyck."

"I know which one you mean."

"Did you pay much for it?"

"Naturally. It is a wonderful example of his work. I would rate it the best he ever did."

"Or Bassete!"

Bassete was consigned to the infernal regions.

"You've got things round the wrong way. The painting you bought at great cost is the Bassete. The other is the Van Dyck."

Veroux stiffened. His beard seemed to jut out at an even steeper angle. "Do you know who I am?"

"I know you're supposed to be an authority in the world of art."

"Supposed to be!" He repeated the words three times, each time with greater irony. "You are uneducated. You are a fool. You are a half-wit."

"Thank you."

"I have a knowledge of Dutch art that is without rival in France. Which means it is ten times as good as anyone's in England. I have studied all my life. I know what I am talking about. I am the final authority."

"Everyone makes mistakes," Blackshirt observed gently.

"I am not everyone. I do not make mistakes. I know every brush-stroke of the Great Master. I know every brush-stroke of all the Great Masters. It was I who determined last year that the painting found in a Dutch farmhouse was not by van Gogh."

"Maybe you were wrong again."

He trembled with rage. "I bracket you with de Marcel! He is a baby who puffs himself up and talks like a man. He claims to know something about Dutch paintings. Yet twice have I caught him out."

"Only once. You must admit he was right about the Bassete and the Van Dyck."

"Admit!" stormed the other. "Over my dead body will I admit it!"

"Adams — the very well-known English critic — saw this painting that you say is a Bassete. He says it is a Van Dyck."

"I do not care."

"Which means it's worth a lot of money." Blackshirt smiled mischievously. "I could sell it in England. Adams would vouch for it."

"Would he? And what use would that be? A man who couldn't tell an El Greco from a Botticelli."

"You know him."

"I've never heard of him. He is an imbecile. He undoubtedly thinks da Vinci painted quite well for a foreigner. This blown-up effigy of a kindergarten art student has the nerve to say my painting is a Van Dyck. He does not listen to what *I* have to say. I am only the final expert in Dutch paintings. I am only known throughout the world."

Blackshirt tried to say something. A hopeless task. His words were instantly submerged.

"Or maybe de Marcel has hired him to instigate this infamous crime. Never has he got over the indignity of being twice wrong. And you, in your stupidity, think this Adams is a greater judge than I am." Veroux was becoming purple in the face as the passions mounted.

"I didn't "

"Be quiet! Have you studied the brushwork of the great Masters? Of course not. Have you studied the futile efforts of Bassete to imitate such work? No. No. Again no. Instead you listen to this... this Adams. Don't think he'll escape with calling me a liar."

"I don't "

"And as for you! For a brief moment your stupid, dull, and insignificant perceptions will be awakened."

The end of the speech came in a flood of French as the struggle to express his violent feelings in English became too much. He jerked forward, grasped the other's arm with his own.

Blackshirt allowed himself to be led over.

"Come here."

Veroux gesticulated in front of the two paintings. He bent down.

"Tell Adams this when you see him. He is not fit to clean a pavement-artist's block of stone. Ask him to shut his trap. Ask de Marcel to shut his trap. Now attend."

He switched on a light which directly illuminated the paintings.

"Here is the brushwork of the Master. Now look at this sloppy mess by the monster who had the impudence to think he could deceive me. Me! What do you find. Chaos! And yet you accept the word of an ignoramus called Adams. Are you at last convinced?"

He turned round.

He was alone

"*Merde!*" he snapped for the second time. "What can one expect from an island where they eat boiled cabbage?"

Verrell unrolled the last sheet of paper, expecting he knew not what. Possibly full directions. Possibly — it didn't matter. He was beyond coherent thought for the moment, for as he unrolled the fifth and final rectangle it disintegrated, as it were, and fluttered over the room like confetti. At least, not over the room; just over the table; and not like confetti, for when he counted the pieces there were only eight. Eight triangles of the same kind of paper, some with a meaningless curving line straggling across. The missing comers...

So it was all a jest; a monstrous practical joke, the practical joke to end all practical jokes, a murderous joke...!

He fingered the triangles idly, then stiffened. He had accidentally placed two together, and the straggling lines joined up. A jig-saw puzzle, of a kind! In a matter of seconds he had put the eight pieces together — and now he had five oblong pieces of tissue-paper of the same size (for the jig-saw puzzle matched the remaining four, but with the addition of its corners), and featuring the same number, 52.

Did the fact of the jig-saw's having all its four corners bear some significance? Did these eight smaller pieces of tissue, these eight triangles, convey the vital clue? For a long time he played with them, but without success. Only after nearly fifteen minutes of concentrated arranging and re-arranging did he suddenly realize the reason for the jig-saw. The eight triangles were the missing corners of the other four tissues; together they made a fifth, and practically identical oblong. Evidently von Steiner must either have been in a terrific hurry when he stuffed the five tissues into the five forged paintings, or else (which was the more reasonable explanation) he must have been short of tissue, and had cut off enough corners from the four whole tissues in order to make a fifth. In which case, what was the significance of size? Did it mean something that the jig-saw was identical in size with the others? He thought that it did, otherwise surely von Steiner would merely have divided one of the other tissues in two.

He laughed as other points became clear in the light of his latest discovery. Not least of all was one which made him realize that he had been a mite too clever, and not only he but the Schmidts and Carr as well. Von Steiner had sent the pictures to his wife with the full knowledge that anything could happen to them in the uncertain conditions of impending defeat. Was it likely, therefore, that the German General would have made the reading of the coded message conditional on his wife's receiving all five Bassetes? — for if he had done so, any one picture's going astray would have deprived her of the fortune. His simple precaution had been to send the message *five* times.

Convinced that any one of the five rectangles would supply the answer to the riddle, Verrell examined them anew, one by one, but to no avail. Only one apparent fact emerged. The number 52 was the vital clue, and there was no need to look beyond that. At last he stubbed out his cigarette, and undressed.

Verrell enjoyed his breakfast by steadfastly refusing to cope with the problem of the tissues until the last drop of coffee had vanished from the cup. Then he returned to the riddle.

The waiter came and asked if there were anything more.

"If I said fifty-two — would it mean anything special to you?"

"In what connection, monsieur?"

"A place in France."

"Whereabouts?"

"That's what I'm trying to find out."

The waiter appeared to think for a few minutes. "I regret, monsieur, but nothing comes to mind."

"How many concentration camps were there during the war?"

"How many — that I cannot say. To us who lived here, one was more than enough. To those who were in them, it was too many."

Verrell frowned. It might be a concentration camp. It might be a regiment number, battalion number... any one of a thousand numbers, he thought wryly. But at least there might be something in the idea.

"Would monsieur be wanting anything else?"

"No, thanks."

The waiter left.

Barring some inspiration the only thing left seemed to be to check through old records. Frankly the thought appalled him. The French were a delightful people. But to extract details of what had happened many years ago would be a feat of superhuman endurance.

In any case it seemed too heavy a solution. Intuition told him it was nothing so complicated. He spread the papers out once more. Could the figures mean anything else? Instead of accepting their face value, perhaps... The possibilities were becoming endless.

By eleven he had had enough of the problem. He went for a walk and on the way stopped at a cafe largely used by tourists. He had gone there because he was not thinking.

Later he strolled in the direction of the Seine. He saw little of what was before him. His brain was hammering away at the problem. Suddenly taking stock of where he was, and checking on the time, he realized he must retrace his steps and think about lunch. He turned suddenly, almost knocked into a couple engrossed in nobody but themselves. He apologized, stepped aside, found himself looking at a bookstall.

There were newspapers in many languages; magazines, some serious, some doubtful; books, guides, maps. When he saw the last he felt like kicking himself. How else did one find one's way around a country? What more natural way of indicating position?

The Michelin guides were famous — and numbered! Each section bore a different number; 52 covered Le Havre, Rouen, Amiens, Dieppe. He bought number 52, unfolded it. The map covered a hell of a lot of country. Too much for the rolls of tissue not to have some hidden significance.

Back at the hotel he spread the map out, superimposed one of the oblongs. Except for the missing corners it was an exact fit. Now what? W^here did he go from there?

Ten minutes later he was home. And as he realized the truth he roared with laughter. It had been a triangular fight. With no holds barred. And all the time each side had had the answer, but by faulty logic had gone on trying to get the five pieces of paper. When he thought of the effort wasted, he laughed the louder. It was a situation which appealed to him.

The solution was in each piece of paper. A microscopic pin-hole at the edge of the top of each figure two. Hidden, until one searched specifically for it, by the darkness of the figure.

And neither he, nor Carr, nor Schmidt had specifically searched for it. For one thing the missing corners had accidentally proved a blind. For another, until he had the fifth piece of paper, there was always the feeling that the next piece would give the solution; and that the piece, or pieces, he already had did not. If only he had thought of the Michelin guides; if only he had… He laughed yet again.

He marked the map with a pencil. The position it gave him was close to a small wood, called the Bois du Chat, four kilometres from the nearest village, Beaudrons, in turn twenty kilometres from Amiens.

He looked at his watch. Had a hasty meal. So hasty it 176 scandalized the *patron* of the small restaurant he had chosen. Then he drove off. Sorry to be leaving Paris so soon; eager to reach the Bois du Chat.

Beaudrons was a very small village. A few houses lined the *pave* road, shutters drawn against the sun. There were two or three small shops, and the inevitable cafe. He stopped at the cafe.

An elderly man came to the table.

"A glass of white wine, please/'

"With pleasure, monsieur."

It was good. So good the price paid seemed ludicrously small.

Soon, after the second glass, he was deep in conversation with the owner. He steered the conversation round to the war years.

"Must have been hell under the occupation?"

"It was. At first their behaviour was correct. Then, one day, they found a German soldier lying in a field stabbed to death. They took six hostages from this small village — and shot them," he ended bitterly.

"Were there many troops round here?"

"There were, monsieur. It became worse and worse as the time went on."

"Did you have a general called von Steiner round this way?"

"I would seem to know the name, but I cannot be sure. I will ask my wife, she will remember."

The old man shuffled inside; returned smiling. "She remembers," he said proudly.

"Was he round here?"

"Yes, monsieur. And now I remember myself. But, of course. He lived at Champiegne, fifteen kilometres from here. He never went short of food, so the story goes! I do know his troops took every animal they could find. It did not matter how old it was."

"He got killed, didn't he?"

"He was shot, not far from here."

"A happy day."

"But yes, monsieur."

Verrell changed the conversation. "Do you know the Bois du Chat?"

"Yes. It is not far from here."

"How do I get there?"

"Along this road and..." The old man was voluble in his explanation. "There was a big *chateau* there, which used to belong to the de Mars family. I can remember..."

When he had implied that his memory was poor, the *patron* had been maligning himself. Only on his third attempt was Verrell able to get away.

The Bois du Chat was a straggly bunch of trees on the top of a small rise, and provided one had enough imagination there was a vague resemblance to the animal in question. A track of sorts led off the main highway and he turned into it, reducing speed to an absolute minimum as the car lurched and bounced on the uneven surface.

The road wound round to the right, passed along a small avenue of trees and came to a halt in front of a building, previously hidden by a hillock, companion to the one on which the woods perched.

At one time the *chateau* must have been a magnificent building. But a stick of high-explosive bombs had reduced it to an empty shell. The walls listed crazily; the inside was a heap of rubble. Verrell realized why, when the *patron* had referred to it in the past tense, there had been sadness in his voice.

He became practical. Somewhere round the ruins, or between them and the woods, the general had cached his loot. Even that rather vague placing might be wrong. The pinprick on the map represented quite a lot of ground.

For a weary hour and a half he scrambled over the ruins, prodding and poking, easing the rubble away where it was possible in an effort to see beneath. The result was negative.

He extended his search to the grounds. Found ample time and reason to swear at the entangled masses of thorns and rank grass which had grown unchecked for years.

Not until he had momentarily stopped his search to enjoy a cigarette, did he meet with any success. It was consistent with the whole affair — the fact that what he was looking for 178

was right under his nose. He had parked his car and gone straight forward to look at the *chateau*. If he had glanced to his right he would have seen the tumbledown gatehouse, and also the top-sides of a small well.

There was no certainty that he had found the hiding-place, but... He crossed to the well, peered down with the aid of his torch.

Very faintly he could see the bottom, and the heap of what looked like rocks piled up on it. A quick check, made visually and by dropping a stone, convinced him the depth was between twenty and thirty feet, and that it was dry.

He needed a rope. Something he had not brought since he had had only the vaguest idea as to what he would find. And even now it was sheer guesswork that the well was the answer.

It was no good asking for rope in the village. That would ensure immediate publicity. He decided to drive back to Amiens where he might find a shop still open, and where his request would cause no comment.

He found a shop on the outskirts of the town. After a while the man behind the counter admitted he had some rope and produced three different sizes. Verrell bought fifty feet of both the thinnest and the stoutest. He returned to his car, drove back to Beaudrons.

Just before the village was a cross-road. A man in a Citroen 2CV came up the minor road, swung into the major road with carefree ease, under the nose of the Healey.

Verrell had no option. He jammed his foot down on the brake-pedal, swung the wheel over. The car bucked and started to skid. He killed the skid, but the effort took him off the road. The nose of the car smacked into a wooden gate, his head slammed onto the steering-wheel. The world exploded into darkness.

Returning to the conscious world was excruciating. First he thought he had a headache which should be recorded as an all-time great. Then he knew he had. It came in waves, growing stronger each time. He lay still, somewhat convinced he was a case for flowers. Then a slight amount of daylight began to filter through and he opened his eyes.

It was a stupid thing to do. A violent ache turned instantly into a raging one.

"Good, he has regained consciousness."

The voice filtered through to his brain. With great effort he opened his eyes again. Things climbed into focus. He was in a sparsely furnished room. At the foot of the bed were two men.

He answered various questions asked by one of the men. He did not know what he was saying. Couldn't have cared less. Finally there was a pause, then he felt the slight prick of a needle. The pain subsided.

The next time he took an interest in the world things were in better perspective. His headache had diminished slightly. On his forehead was a bump that exploratory fingers soon determined was of great size.

"Monsieur, how are you?" The speaker was the owner of the little cafe in Beaudrons. He soon introduced himself as Jules.

A meal was brought. It consisted of nothing but a light broth, nevertheless tasted delicious.

While Verrell was eating — or drinking — Jules chatted away, occasionally pausing to make certain he was not tiring his guest; continuing before he received an answer.

"And Jules — he has the same name as I, but since he is not a Courbet there is no difficulty — swears he will never forgive himself. To drive out into the other road as he did! But as I have said to him many times 'One day you will have an accident'. And, now, he has!"

Verrell did not like to spoil the satisfaction with which the last sentence was uttered, by remarking that Jules had not had an accident. He had merely caused one since, apparently, he had escaped without even a scratch to his car.

The doctor arrived.

"Good morning, Monsieur Verrell. How do you feel?"

He made a quick examination.

"You are lucky. Everything is well. With luck you can get out of bed in perhaps four days."

"Not before?"

"On no account. Now, can I send any message to England for you?"

"I don't think so, thanks."

"Then I shall be in tomorrow some time. Perhaps you would like me to bring you an English newspaper? I can get one when I pass through the town."

"Thanks a lot. I should."

The doctor left. Jules reported that the other Jules was repairing the Healey.

"You were very fortunate, monsieur I You ran into a mechanic of the first order."

Verrell gravely agreed that he had been exceedingly lucky.

The day passed. Most of the time he slept. Which did not prevent his sleeping right through the night.

The doctor arrived as he was finishing his breakfast. Examined his head.

"It is very much quieter. In three days at the most, you may rise. Perhaps two. Forgive me now, please, but I must continue on my way. Before I go, however, here is the paper I promised you. I trust it is one of which you approve?"

It was the air-mail edition of the *Telegraph*.

"Very many thanks."

"A pleasure." The doctor left, with a courtesy unblunted by a National Health scheme.

Verrell read the front page. Turned to the centre of the newspaper. The first thing he saw was a short paragraph which made him wince. It reported that Richard Verrell, the novelist, had been injured in a car accident in the north of France while on a motoring trip. It went so far as to give the name of the village.

The paper was dated the previous day. Twenty-four hours had passed since the news of his whereabouts had been published. He threw back the bedclothes, stood up. Pain returned with a rush. For a moment it was touch and go. Then things sorted themselves out sufficiently for him to dress. He left the room to look for Jules. Both of them.

Chapter Seventeen

Jules wasted five minutes trying to make his guest see reason. In the end he gave up the struggle with a shrug of his shoulders, 'phoned the other Jules and asked for the car to be brought round immediately.

'Immediately' became three-quarters of an hour. Then the deep-throated roar of the car's exhaust announced the arrival of the other Jules.

"Monsieur, I have brought your car along. I have straightened the front as you will see. I cannot tell you how desolated I am — never have I done such a thing before!"

The further flood of words delayed Verrell until he was forced to cut them short. He climbed into his car, drove off.

As soon as he reached the *chateau* he set to work. From the back of the car he took the two lengths of rope. He knotted the thicker at three-foot intervals, tied one end of it round the base of a tree growing to one side of the well. He dropped the other end down the well. The thinner length of rope he left on the ground.

He lowered his legs down the well, took his weight with his hands. Very slowly he descended, roundly cursing his head each time the rope swung and brought him against the sides of the shaft with a sharp jerk. Just when it seemed that one more blow would cause an oversize explosion in his thrumming brain, his feet touched bottom.

His stand was precarious, perched as he was on top of rubble. Large chunks of concrete which appeared to have been thrown down haphazardly served, he realized, a purpose. To conceal a small cleft in the brickwork at one side of the well. A fact he found only after strenuous effort.

He squeezed through the cleft, half-crawled, half-stumbled along a rough passageway which turned sharply to the right almost as soon as he entered it.

Twenty feet farther along he reached a space which might have been natural, but which had every appearance of having been completed by man. It was big, though not lofty. At the far side were a number of packing-cases.

Within half an hour Verrell knew approximately the value 182 of the loot he had found. It was incredible. There was jewellery of every kind. In such quantities it became increasingly difficult to believe it could all be genuine. There was a rope of pearls which made him whistle with delight. There were cases filled with nothing but gold; cases filled with paintings.

Even though the General had spent several years looting, it was still incredible that he could have amassed so much. By contrast, the Freshman collection was a small sideline.

He had a second look at the pearls. They were large, beautifully matched and graded. Even in the torchlight their warmth was magnificent.

"I'm glad we aren't too late."

He switched off the torch. Immediately a powerful beam of light outlined him.

"We've arrived at the right moment in more ways than one. All the dirty work done for us. You're too generous... Mr. Blackshirt."

A hurricane lamp was lit. It illuminated the chamber with its soft light. Verrell turned. Carr was grinning, a gun held negligently in his right hand. Seeton was five feet to his right.

"You're early," answered Verrell cheerfully.

"I bet we are! Any time within the next few days would have been early. That's what comes of getting your name in the papers."

"Wasn't any wish of mine I can assure you. My head's still darned painful."

"Don't worry about it too much!" Carr grinned.

"Thanks."

Seeton spoke jeeringly. "Always the gentleman."

"You've almost been clever," murmured Carr in the ensuing pause.

"At the risk of annoying your friend again — thank you." He bowed.

"Don't take it as too much of a compliment. Part of the trouble was my fault. I thought you were just a nosey author. Thought it was Jackson who stole the painting from the Old Masters' Gallery. Didn't connect up with you. Nearly a fatal mistake."

"Don't blame yourself too much."

"I don't. If I'd been on the spot right from the beginning things wouldn't have gone as they did. And if I'd known you were Blackshirt I'd have given the devil his due."

"You seem convinced I'm this cracksman?"

Seeton chuckled.

Carr continued gazing at him with a mixture of emotions. Hatred and jealousy were struggling with admiration.

"Jackson didn't break into the Gallery. Strange to think I ever reckoned he had enough guts. Only one person could have played it the way it was. Blackshirt. The same person who broke into my house."

Verrell made a slight movement to ease his foot.

For several seconds the other two tensed. Then relaxed as they realized Verrell was not making an effort to escape.

"You took a lot of my money," continued Carr. "And the squares of paper which meant so much and cost a hell of a lot to get."

"Apart from the first one, your money was wasted!"

"How...?"

"Unfortunately," said Verrell with a straight face, "every one of the five pieces of paper gave the answer."

Carr digested the fact. He realized what it meant. That he had had the solution a long time before. That if he had realized the fact, he could have scooped the kitty. He swore.

Verrell laughed with genuine humour. "It's rather funny, if one stops to think about it! Everybody rushing "

"Keep the funny act to yourself," Carr snapped. "Maybe you think you've been brilliant?"

"I wouldn't go that far," replied the other modestly.

"I don't care how far you'd go." Carr was rapidly losing his temper. "This time you've come to the end of the line. Maybe I didn't realize what was what — but I would have got the answer much quicker if you hadn't been around."

"I'm not certain that that makes sense."

"I can't stand much more of this," snapped Seeton. "Rub him out and get on with the job."

"Patience," responded Carr, thereby ignoring his own behaviour a moment before. He switched the conversation. "What's the stuff like?" He indicated the cases.

"Unbelievable."

"There's supposed to be a fortune here."

"More than one."

"In that case, Blackshirt, I can thank you for something. Saved us a lot of mental worry. Your crash was inspired/'

"You wouldn't say that if you had my head."

"If I had your head I'd "

"Shut up, Seeton." Carr cut short a possible witticism. "I'm going to have a look. I've been chasing this little lot for more months than I care to remember. Move over to the right, Blackshirt, and get up against the wall. Seeton, drop him the moment he makes a move."

"It'll be a pleasure."

Verrell slowly did as he was bid.

"That's far enough. Hold your hands over your head and keep them there."

Carr waited until his order was carried out. Then he crossed the floor of the cavern and greedily searched through the crates.

"My God!" he murmured. "It's ten times what I thought."

Seeton leaned forward trying to get a glimpse of the wealth they had at last reached.

"Watch Blackshirt. Never mind this," snapped Carr.

"He's all right."

"See he stays that way." A pause. "If this isn't worth ten thousand I'm a Dutchman." He held up a diamond ring.

"What a pity you'll never be certain of your nationality," broke in a new voice. A woman's voice.

"This is where I came in," said Verrell. "If someone had brought some tea we could have a tea party." He smiled at Paula Schmidt.

Carr and Seeton stood frozen. The former sideways to the entrance, where the woman was standing. The latter with his back to it.

"How are you?" asked Verrell.

"Drop your guns," she said, in her amazingly flat voice.

Seeton had more courage than sense. He whirled round on his feet, died before he completed the turn. The bullet smacked into his chest, threw him sideways.

"I'm glad it wasn't you," she said to Carr.

He licked his lips. Had to ask, "Why?"

"I said drop your gun."

He did so.

"Because I've been wanting to meet you ever since you killed my husband."

"Keep going, Paula," suggested Verrell. "They've been threatening to do lots of things to me. Now it's your turn."

"I'm surprised to find you still here! I thought you had more sense. My husband would not have been killed but for your telling Carr where to find him."

"Don't blame me for that. Not that I should lose any sleep if I had."

"I wish you'd brought your girl friend along."

"I bet you do. Keep you amused for days and days. Don't know if you'd heard, Carr, but this little woman ran a health resort during the war. One of those places complete with gas ovens."

There was no doubt as to what was happening to Carr. He was folding up. His face had gone white. A nervous twitch started at the side of his mouth.

"Don't let that worry you. We're two against one!" Verrell laughed. He genuinely seemed to be enjoying himself.

Paula looked at him with respect. "As I said once before, I almost like you. It's a pity we shall not be able to enjoy one another's company much longer."

"For once I'm inclined to agree with you." He half bowed: ironically.

"Stop this blasted rot and do something," suddenly shouted Carr.

"What, for instance?"

There was no answer.

"No good your complaining too much! You started it all. Paula's merely followed in your footsteps."

Carr's nerve cracked. He charged straight at the small opening which led to the outside world of sanity.

Paula hardly seemed to take aim. But when she fired the other fell to the ground as his legs folded underneath him. The thin tendrils of acrid smoke floated upwards and joined those already hanging on the roof.

She walked across to the wounded man. The shadows on the walls moved in step. Without passion she kicked the smashed thigh.

Carr's thin scream of pain made Verrell wince. "Leave the poor devil alone," he snapped.

She looked at him with faint amusement. "As always, that fatal streak of softness. It will get you nowhere. The curse of the English."

"It didn't prevent our winning the war!"

"We were betrayed."

"Twaddle," he replied.

Her face tightened. She lined the revolver up with his stomach.

He looked at her with a mocking expression.

"In a minute. There is no hurry," she said.

"You haven't finished with Carr?"

"Perhaps."

"Then what?"

"Then I shall return to Germany. When I have sold this treasure I shall be rich. Very rich. I shall spend the money wisely." She was speaking her thoughts aloud.

"Sounds as though you're going to invest in another interior decorator."

She did not catch the allusion for a few seconds. When she did she walked across the floor, slammed the muzzle of the gun into his middle. Then, twice, she slashed his shins with her pointed shoes.

The pain was intense.

"Your manners are appalling," she said, back once more in the centre of the cavern.

"I wouldn't recommend yours."

"Small matter."

She noticed that Carr was dragging himself across the floor. Casually, she sent two more bullets smacking into his body. He died quite quickly.

For a fleeting second Verrell realized that two men had come down to the cavern knowing that he and Blackshirt were one and the same person. That he must be, because of the theft from Veroux. They were both dead. A great comfort — with Paula around.

"Have you examined those?" She indicated the crates.

"Roughly. There might even be something to leave to your grandchildren."

"You claim nothing for yourself?"

He smiled. "Would it do much good?"

She shrugged her shoulders. "These things have to be."

He laughed.

"What is amusing you?"

He never had time to answer. From above there came a shout. It echoed backwards and forwards in the cavern. It was eerie to hear the name of 'Verrell' repeated again and again.

"Somebody has at last brought the tea." He relaxed imperceptibly.

"Who is it?" Her forefinger tightened round the trigger.

"My guardian angel!"

"You fool! Must you joke yourself to death? Who was it?"

"How the devil should I know? I wasn't expecting callers until dinner-time."

Again his name was called out. This time he recognized the voice. Wright had backed his hunches to the limit.

"Will you answer?" She was about to fire.

"Careful — don't forget you've got to get out yourself."

She realized the fact. Like a good general she came to an immediate decision.

"Go forward and through the passage. Stand at the bottom of the shaft. Find out who is there, tell him to leave. I shall be behind you. If necessary I shall shoot. Maybe I shall suffer, but it will bring you no comfort."

"Your logic is unassailable," he admitted.

"It's meant to be. Start moving."

He stepped round the wall, hunched up and moved along the passage. He could hear her behind him. He turned the comer and reached the thin haze of daylight coming from above.

"Start talking," she whispered.

He looked up. Wright was peering down from above.

"You want me?"

A torch was switched on and the beam caught him.

"Of course I want you. Why the hell d'you think I was shouting? Come up and stop playing smugglers. I've got half the French police-force waiting."

Verrell recognized the message underlining the jerked sentences. He had found the loot. It was clever of him. It would be still cleverer of him to leave it precisely where it was.

"Didn't expect to see you around," he answered.

"Never mind the platitudes. Get the hell out of there. You're supposed to be in bed."

"You haven't long/' Paula whispered.

"I can't come up right now/' he replied.

"Don't be a fool. Can't you understand — or has the crash weakened your brain?" Wright was impatient. It had taken much fast talking to smooth things out. Now the other was threatening to ruin everything. Couldn't he realize he was beaten?

"Go off and have a meal! I'm much too busy exploring stalagmites and stalag-types."

Wright jumped to it at once. The reference showed Verrell was not playing the fool, however much he might be smiling. To date there had only been two Germans mixed up in the affair. One was dead: finally. Then Paula was below.

"Warm down there?" he asked.

"It is getting quite hot/' Verrell answered.

Wright had the picture. Somewhere along the line a gun was trained on Blackshirt's back.

"Is it dark down there?" he asked.

"It is. Especially when there's no light."

Verrell wondered if the other would get the hint. So delicate as to be almost invisible. Paula had left the hurricane lamp behind — had followed without a torch.

Wright stood up, took off his coat in a series of jerky movements as he tried to keep the torch trained on the figure below. He held the coat in his hands. "You'll be ready to move when I am?"

"I shall."

Wright switched off the torch, flung himself forward over the mouth of the well, used the coat to cut off the last chink of light. He thought it would be just too bad if bullets started coming upwards.

Verrell moved with split-second timing. As the light went out he jumped upwards. He gripped the rope that lay down the side of the well.

Paula was caught unawares by the speed with which things happened. For a full second she was motionless. Then she lowered the revolver and fired.

As the sound of the shot echoed away there came a scream of pain. She smiled flatly. While she was at the foot of the well help could not come. She moved forward, ready to fire the instant there was any movement.

She took one step, then another. Her left hand still met nothing. She moved again. She felt the side of the well in front of her. As she grasped the fact that there was no body, a solid weight landed on top of her. She crumpled up, lay still.

Verrell painfully picked himself up. The other had a head which could only be described as hard.

"Wright!" he shouted.

The man above whipped the coat away, switched on the torch. He eased his pent-up feelings with a sigh of relief. The scream had been too realistic.

"Can you come up now?" he asked sarcastically.

"Once you've removed this beautiful hunk of womanhood."

"Tie the rope round her."

Verrell tied a noose round the middle of the groaning woman, already returning to consciousness. He called up. Paula was taken upwards. He climbed up the rope himself, as soon as the end was returned from above.

"Always causing trouble," grunted Wright.

"Why blame me?" he asked with pained voice.

The other laughed shortly.

"I'm afraid there are a couple more bodies below," he said.

"See what I mean!"

"I didn't shoot them."

"More's the pity. Could have had you slapped straight in gaol. Now it's their worry right from the beginning. Damned if I'm going to explain things." Wright indicated the small knot of French police.

"Hope they enjoy it."

"Anything else down there?"

"A few oddments."

Wright looked at him coldly. Abruptly he turned. "Your valuables are below, Monsieur Therbaut."

"A thousand thanks. A " He was cut short. Paula, struggling viciously, shouted something at the top of her voice.

The two men holding her cursed.

"Who is she?" asked the Frenchman.

"Paula Schmidt," replied Wright.

There was a silence. Impressive. Every pair of French eyes regarded the struggling woman.

"Paula Schmidt," said Therbaut. He caressed his chin. He 190 repeated the name carefully. "For many years, too many, we have been looking for her." He took two steps forward and addressed her with French theatrics. "You have a date, madame, which this time you will keep!"

She cursed.

Wright spoke to Verrell. "Come over here a moment." The two men walked away.

"I want you to get this straight. I've made certain that everybody understands you've found all this stuff so you can hand it over to the French police."

"Have you?"

"Yes. They may even give you the Legion of Honour, if you're lucky. But…" Wright's smile was kindly. "To make certain everything's above board I'll just remove this from your kind custody." He removed a small bag from the other's right-hand pocket.

Verrell was crestfallen. "Of all the…," he muttered at length. "You're becoming far too clever."

Wright dropped the bag into his own coat.

Verrell went on: "What about all the trouble I've been to? I nearly got blown to bits five times over down there." "Shouldn't play with fire."

"If it hadn't been for me, nobody would have got a thing." "Then you can henceforward regard yourself as a philanthropist. Ought to make you feel good. Isn't that worth something?"

"I'm damned if I shan't go back and have a stab at the Bank of England! This was supposed to pay for a holiday." "I'll tell them you're coming."

He sighed. "It's a grim world."

"Oh! Nearly forgot. I met a doctor who was running round in circles trying to find you. You're meant to be in bed still. Suppose you return and climb in between the sheets. You can buy me a drink later."

"Arsenic," suggested Verrell.

He did as he was bid. Walked to his car, drove off. Now he came to reflect, he was feeling the effects…

He stopped at the cafe and handsomely recompensed the *patron*, refused to listen to the doctor's warnings which were relayed with much vigour.

He drove towards the coast. He sang. He had reason to.

In his inside pocket was a rope of pearls that defied description. Something had told him that Wright would never believe he had come up empty-handed from such treasure trove.

He sang still louder. With luck he would be back in time to take Diana out to dinner. She must be wondering what was going on, he reflected.

If you enjoyed Salute to Blackshirt, please share your thoughts on Amazon by leaving a review.

For more free and discounted eBooks every week, sign up to the Endeavour Press newsletter.

Follow us on Twitter and Instagram.

35878348R00108

Printed in Poland
by Amazon Fulfillment
Poland Sp. z o.o., Wrocław